D0549811

TRIPPING OVER
SKYSCRAPERS

Books by Wendy Lee Nentwig
from Bethany House Publishers

———— ✳ ————

Unmistakably Cooper Ellis

1. *Tripping Over Skyscrapers*
2. *Moonstruck in Manhattan*

TRIPPING OVER SKYSCRAPERS

WENDY LEE NENTWIG

BETHANY HOUSE PUBLISHERS
MINNEAPOLIS, MINNESOTA 55438

Tripping Over Skyscrapers
Copyright © 1998
Wendy Lee Nentwig

Cover illustration by William Graf
Cover design by Lookout Design Group

Unless otherwise identified, Scripture quotations are from the HOLY
BIBLE, NEW INTERNATIONAL VERSION®. Copyright © 1973, 1978,
1984 by International Bible Society. Used by permission of
Zondervan Publishing House. All rights reserved. The "NIV" and
"New International Version" trademarks are registered in the United
States Patent and Trademark Office by International Bible Society.
Use of either trademark requires the permission of International
Bible Society.

All rights reserved. No part of this publication may be reproduced,
stored in a retrieval system, or transmitted in any form or by any
means—electronic, mechanical, photocopying, recording, or
otherwise—without the prior written permission of the publisher and
copyright owners.

Published by Bethany House Publishers
A Ministry of Bethany Fellowship International
11300 Hampshire Avenue South
Minneapolis, Minnesota 55438
www.bethanyhouse.com

Printed in the United States of America by
Bethany Press International, Minneapolis, Minnesota 55438

Library of Congress Cataloging-in-Publication Data

CIP data applied for

ISBN 0–7642–2065–9   CIP

For my sister,
Barbara Holmstrom.

A wonderful mother, sister, and friend.
I wish we hadn't wasted so much time in high school,
but I'm glad we're making up for it now.

WENDY LEE NENTWIG is a graduate of Biola University and spent her college years studying journalism before launching into a diverse magazine career, including stints with *Virtue* and *Seventeen*. In addition to her journalistic accomplishments, Wendy has worked extensively with teens, both overseas and at home, and has published two young adult novels, *Freshman Blues* and *Spring Break*. A born traveler, Wendy currently calls Tennessee home, where she is Managing Editor of *Aspire* magazine.

COOPER ELLIS WAS DETERMINED not to be last today. Not again. Pushing her way through the crowded halls after fourth period and sprinting down the stairs, she raced to her locker and furiously spun the dial on her combination lock. Pulling the door open so forcefully that it slammed against the locker next to it with an echoing metallic clang, she stuffed her books inside, grabbed her lunch, and took off in the direction of the cafeteria.

Her heart was pounding from the workout, and wisps of her straight, dark hair kept falling into her gray eyes, but she was determined to beat them this time. Certain she had done just that, Cooper triumphantly skidded around the final corner, the finish line within reach, when two figures—one male and one female—appeared out of nowhere. They loomed menacingly, blocking her entrance to the lunchroom. At the sight of them a low groan escaped from somewhere deep inside Cooper, and she sagged against the cold concrete wall to catch her breath.

Leaning against opposite ends of the doorjamb were her two best friends, looking as if they hadn't rushed at all and had still managed to beat her to the cafeteria with minutes to spare.

"Some friends you are," Cooper called to the pair between huffs and puffs. "You could at least look winded!"

"Your time's improving," Claire offered helpfully after consulting her watch.

Their friend Alex wasn't so generous. "Thank you for playing last-one-to-the-cafeteria-has-to-wait-in-the-Coke-machine-line!" he announced in an annoying game-show-host voice.

Cooper, still breathing hard, just glared at him, but he wasn't deterred.

Clutching an imaginary microphone, he continued. "Claire, tell our friend Cooper what she's won!" When Claire just rolled her eyes at Alex, he went ahead without her. "Cooper Ellis, you've just won an all-expenses-paid trip to . . . the cafeteria! That's right! You'll be traveling to the beautiful Hudson High cafeteria, where you will be given the honor of waiting in line for beverages not just for yourself but for your thirsty friends, as well! But wait—that's not all. When you're all done, you'll be having lunch in the scenic east courtyard!"

The girls left Alex talking to himself in the hall while they made their way into the packed cafeteria.

"It's not fair!" Cooper whined to Claire, hoping for a little sympathy. "You guys both know there is absolutely no way I can make it from the bio lab—which just happens to be upstairs and at the farthest possible end of the hall—to the cafeteria before either of you. And of course you both lucked out with honors English fourth period, which is so close you might as well just have class *in* the cafeteria."

Alex had caught up with them by now, catching the last of her speech, but he didn't look impressed. In fact, both friends wore amused expressions, and Cooper realized she wasn't getting anywhere. Sighing dramatically, she pointed out what they all already knew: "I am doomed to be the designated beverage-buyer for the entire semester!"

Claire and Alex just laughed and handed over their quarters. "That's one Diet Coke and one root beer, miss," Alex called after Cooper as if she were a waitress and he were placing an order.

Like she needed reminding. The trio had been eating together for years. Cooper watched her friends exit the cafeteria through the huge back doors that opened onto the enclosed courtyard before shuffling off to join the endless line at her school's only soda machine. She'd be sure to toss Alex's root beer in the air a few times before delivering it.

Cooper hadn't really expected any sympathy. Not that her friends were unfeeling, but last semester Claire had gym class right before lunch, and even when she made the sacrifice of not drying her long, wavy brown hair or touching up her makeup, she was still last to the lunchroom every day but one. Cooper remembered Claire's often-dripping hair and how her friend spent many lunch periods reapplying blush or eye shadow to her pretty olive skin in between quick bites of lunch.

Alex had had his turn, too. All of freshman year had been his turn, actually. In fact, Cooper was sure that if the rule hadn't been Alex's idea in the first place, he would have protested loudly. It *had* been his plan, though, and he was so proud of coming up with the idea that whoever was last to the cafeteria each day had to wait in the drink line. Of course, he came up with that brainstorm before he consulted his schedule and realized just how far away his freshman history class was from the lunchroom. But since he had come up with the plan and the girls had only reluctantly agreed to comply, he had no choice but to be "drink boy" (as they dubbed him after only a few weeks of high school) all through ninth grade.

Now, at long last, it was Cooper's turn. She knew it had to happen eventually. For a fleeting moment she considered spending the semester eating lunch with some other sophomores, *any* other sophomores, but quickly dismissed it. She couldn't imagine eating with anyone else and honestly couldn't recall a time when she had done so. She and Claire had eaten together forever it seemed. Their parents had been friends since before the girls were born, and Cooper and Claire were practically raised as sisters, which was nice since they were both only children. They even lived in the same apartment building on New York City's Upper West Side.

How Alex had joined them was a bit more complex, and Cooper couldn't remember it without smiling. One day in seventh grade, looking for a diversion in health class, Alex passed a note to the boy who sat in front of him telling him that he had heard Cooper liked him. This kept both boys busy for the rest of the period passing the note back and forth, adding new bits of information (most of it false) as they went. It was a common seventh grade practice, and Alex didn't think much of it until after school when a furious Cooper with a reluctant Claire in tow followed him home.

On the sidewalk in front of his apartment building, Cooper towered over Alex and loudly confronted him. Of course, he denied having anything to do with the whole thing, but he cowered anyway as Cooper stood a good six inches taller than he did. The denial was barely out of his mouth when Cooper thrust a crumpled piece of notebook paper in his face. Alex sank to the curb in defeat at the sight of this hard evidence. In the end, Cooper wouldn't leave until he had promised to tell the boy first thing the next morning that he made the whole thing up and to make it clear that Cooper wouldn't like him if he were the last seventh grader on earth (even though that wasn't exactly true). Alex kept his word, and the next day at lunch he found the girls and gave them a full report, then pulled out his sandwich and joined them. He had been eating lunch with them ever since.

As the quarters *clink-clink-clinked* their way into the inner depths of the Coke machine, Cooper realized that despite their quirks there were no two people she'd rather stand in line for than Claire and Alex. God sure knew what He was doing when He brought them together. Holding on to that happy thought and three ice-cold drinks, she made her way out to their usual spot in the courtyard where Claire waved to her.

"It's about time," Alex mock-complained, running his fingers through his messy brown hair. It didn't help, though. He always had that rumpled gas-station-attendant look about him. It was probably a combination of the thrift store shirts and the big black work boots he always wore.

Cooper gave his drink a few good shakes before tossing it to him. Then she gently handed Claire her Diet Coke before popping open her own.

"Hey!" Alex protested while simultaneously tapping the top of his unopened can with his fingers, trying to settle its explosive contents.

"What?" Cooper asked innocently, tucking her long legs under her and smoothing her short corduroy skirt down over her tights.

"Oh nothing," Alex conceded with a shrug, but not before pointing his root beer in her direction.

"You wouldn't dare," Cooper challenged, but even before she finished her sentence she knew he would. She was still taller than he was, but only by a few inches now. And since seventh grade, Alex had learned to more than hold his own in their mini-battles. He was just about to pull the pop-top when a pair of shiny penny loafers came to an abrupt stop in front of the group. Each of the three craned their necks to see who the shoes belonged to.

"Hey, Mr. Danenhauer! What can we do for you?" Cooper asked, her enthusiasm stemming more from her relief at avoiding a root beer shower than from any genuine fondness for their honors English teacher.

"Good afternoon, Cooper," he replied, then turned his gaze upon Claire and Alex. "Actually, I was hoping to talk to you two after class, but you raced out so fast I didn't get a chance," the teacher explained. "I thought perhaps the building was on fire."

They did hurry to the cafeteria after all! Cooper realized and gave her friends a pointed look. Neither one would meet her gaze, but she thought she detected a slight smile playing on Alex's lips. Knowing she'd never get them to admit it, she focused back in on what Mr. Danenhauer was saying.

" . . . so while I don't have a problem with the content of your reading group, per se, in order to get the extra credit, you are going to need to open it up to the rest of the student body."

That last sentence was enough to let Cooper know that Mr. Danenhauer wasn't bringing them good news.

"But, Mr. Danenhauer, we've never told anyone they couldn't come!" Cooper protested.

"But you've never really invited them, either," he corrected. "One announcement over the school PA system the week before you started is hardly what I'd call an advertising campaign."

"Well . . ." Alex stalled.

"I'm not interested in excuses. I want to see some signs up and the group listed on the events board before your next meeting if you want that extra credit. Understood?"

All three heads bobbed in agreement without looking up. They knew it had been too good to last. It was too easy. The three of them had been reading through different C. S. Lewis books and discussing them informally since freshman year. When Mr. Danenhauer offered extra credit to any students who started a literature-related club on campus, Alex convinced the girls to make their little reading group official. They were doing the work already, so why not get credit for it? And they would need some activities to put on their college applications.

Cooper was hesitant. They had started reading the books as a sort of alternative Bible study. The church they attended had absolutely no youth group, and they were looking for something to supplement the general sermons they got each Sunday. Turning it into a club would mean they'd have to change the whole focus, Cooper had protested. But Claire was undecided on the whole issue, which made it easier for Alex to eventually win them over with his promise that if they didn't like the way it turned out they'd go back to how things were before. So with a single vague announcement over the PA system and a room request turned in to the front office, the reading group became official. And much to Cooper's amazement, nothing *had* changed—except that now they received English extra credit and were allowed to meet each week in the comfy environs of the second-floor student lounge. Until now, that is.

"What are we going to do?" Cooper asked, removing a plastic container of cold pasta from her *Partridge Family* lunch box. "I knew we should have just left things the way they were!"

"Don't be so sure of that," Alex warned, a familiar glint in his green eyes.

"Oh no, not another plan, Alex! Please, anything but that," Cooper pleaded, her hands raised in surrender.

"You remember last time," Claire warned.

"What? What happened last time?"

The girls looked at him, incredulous.

"How can you *not* remember what happened?" Cooper queried. "The Great Chorale Debacle? You thought we needed to broaden our horizons a little and convinced us to try out?"

When Cooper looked over at Alex to see if any of this was sounding familiar, he just shrugged his shoulders and stared blankly as if he didn't recall a thing. She wasn't about to let him off the hook so easily, though.

"Maybe this will jog your memory. We were all so bad, so *completely* unmusical, that Mrs. Morgan asked us to refrain from even venturing into the music wing for fear we'd somehow contaminate those who do have talent!"

That was all it took to get Alex to jump to his own defense.

"Don't you think that's a bit of an exaggeration? True, she asked us not to sing ever again in her presence or near anyone else in chorale, but she said it in the nicest possible way. And I'm sure if we wanted to just *attend* a performance we'd be welcome. Well . . . maybe," Alex said, not sounding at all certain.

"You got us banned from an entire wing of the school!"

Claire pointed out. "That is not an exaggeration!"

At that, Cooper chimed in. "And there are fifty people roaming this campus right now who will always remember us as the dorks who sang that incredibly lame version of the *Scooby-Doo* theme song at tryouts. It's no wonder I don't have a boyfriend!"

"Okay, okay, okay! I admit it wasn't the best choice of music or of extracurricular activities, but I take no responsibility for your less-than-active date-life. Maybe if you weren't six feet tall! And I think I've apologized for that little chorale episode more than once, so can we please stop living in the past?"

"We're trying, Alex. Believe me, we're trying," an exasperated Cooper explained. "It's a little hard, though, when history keeps threatening to repeat itself. And by the way, I'm a very petite five ten, so there!"

"Whatever. You're still taller than ninety-nine percent of the sophomore class, but that's not the issue here. You guys have to admit the reading group is something we know how to do. We're *good* at it. And maybe this is God's way of forcing us to get out of our comfort zone. I mean, if we advertise and people actually come, we could really have a positive impact on this campus," Alex said enthusiastically.

"How do we know it's *God* pushing us out of our comfort zone and not you? Hmm?" Claire wanted to know.

"I can see how you'd be concerned, but c'mon, our pretty much anti-religious school administration has practically given us permission to hold a Bible study on campus, and now they're forcing us to invite other students! I'm good, but I'm not that good. The credit for this one has to go to the Big Guy," Alex said, pointing his finger up in the air.

"Well," Cooper said reluctantly to Claire, "it pains me to

admit this, but he might just be right . . . for once."

Claire shrugged in mild agreement.

"You guys won't be sorry," Alex gushed. "This is going to be so great!"

Cooper was already sorry, but it was too late. Alex was in planning mode.

"We'll have to come up with a concept for the ads by this weekend so we can get to work on them. And don't worry, I can put them up during my free period on Monday. Then I guess we can go over the schedule for next week's meeting during lunch, but it might be good to get together the night before for a quick run-through."

He was talking to himself, but Cooper couldn't help jumping in. "Uh, Alex?" she said, waving her hand in front of his face to snap him out of his little organizational fit. "It's a reading group, remember? What is there to plan? We read. We discuss. We go home. That's the beauty of it: no planning necessary."

"That was fine when it was just the three of us. But if we're going to have some new members, I think we need to make some decisions," Alex explained.

"What kind of decisions?" Cooper asked reluctantly as she stuffed several used plastic bags back in her lunch box before snapping it shut.

"Like what are we going to call the group, for starters?"

"I don't know why we have to call it anything," Cooper protested, but this time Claire took Alex's side.

"It does make sense to give the group a name," she admitted. "It wouldn't hurt."

"This is exactly what I was afraid of," Cooper charged. "All these changes are going to ruin our spontaneous little reading group, and when they do, I just want it on the record that I was against this from the start."

"Duly noted," Alex retorted sarcastically. "Now, do you have any suggestions for names or not?"

"No," Cooper grudgingly admitted.

"Well, I guess Claire and I will just have to come up with something on our own," he announced, looking to Claire for a little moral support.

"Fine," Cooper said a little touchily.

"Fine," Alex echoed.

Before another harsh word could be spoken—or better yet, any sort of truce reached—the bell rang, summoning everyone to fifth period. As Cooper stashed her lunch box in her locker and grabbed her books for geometry class, she couldn't calm the uneasy feeling in the pit of her stomach or quiet the nagging voice in her head that told her her life was about to change . . . whether she liked it or not.

ON THE SURFACE, at least, everything still seemed normal. The three friends met at Cooper's on Friday night for their weekly videofest just like they always did. Movie-obsessed Alex brought three tapes that he felt fit the theme he had chosen for the evening: movies that were better than the books on which they were based. Alex always picked the theme, but the girls didn't mind since he knew more about movies than anyone they had ever met. He planned to go to film school after they graduated, and the girls had no doubt he would be a famous director someday.

By 11:00 P.M. they had only made it through *To Kill a Mockingbird*, but that wasn't surprising since they always began the night with more movies than they could possibly watch. And, of course, Alex was always pausing the tape to re-watch his favorite parts, which only added to their running time.

After seeing young Scout dressed in a ham costume for the fifth time, Cooper and Claire headed to the kitchen to make some more caramel popcorn, shouting "PORK!" as they went. It was Scout's only line in the school pageant, and the whole scene was so absurd that the first time they saw it they were convulsed with laughter. Alex had to pause the movie until they could compose themselves. Now they only had to utter the word and the laughter returned. Cooper was sure she would never look at bacon in quite the same way. Then again, she had felt that way after seeing *Babe*, too.

As Cooper pulled the plain popcorn from the microwave and added the caramel goop to the bag of just-popped kernels, her parents returned home from dinner, peeking their heads into the kitchen.

"Hi, honey. Hi, Claire," Mrs. Ellis said while straightening her velvet-trimmed blazer, even though she was home now and it was just them. Cooper knew she wouldn't kick off her high-heeled pumps, either, until she got ready for bed. Cooper's dad, on the other hand, had already loosened his tie and was slipping the silk noose from around his neck. With his sandy brown hair falling across his forehead, he reached into the popcorn bag and managed to grab a few clean kernels.

"Hey, you just ate!" Cooper chided as she swatted at her dad's hand.

"That doesn't mean I don't have room for popcorn," Mr. Ellis explained as he tossed a kernel in the air and caught it in his mouth.

"Jack, leave the kids alone," Mrs. Ellis said, tugging gently at her husband's sleeve.

"Enjoy the rest of your movie-watching," he called over his shoulder as Cooper's parents made their way down the hall.

"And be careful with that caramel corn on the furniture," Mrs. Ellis added.

As if Cooper didn't know better than to drizzle caramel all over her mother's pale, stiff couch. And it was her *mother's* couch, not hers or her father's. Cooper would have chosen something more inviting, with big, soft cushions you could sink into and a plaid pattern that hid stains. But her mother had very strong ideas about furniture. In fact, she had very strong ideas about everything, and they rarely were in line with her daughter's.

Cooper's mental fog lifted when Alex entered the kitchen, helping himself to a drink from the Ellises' refrigerator, which he knew almost as well as his own. He popped it open before sitting backward in one of the stiff-backed chairs gathered around the kitchen table.

"So do you need help making signs this weekend?" Claire asked Alex, catching Cooper a little off guard.

"I was planning on doing them tomorrow," Alex explained. "You want to come over in the afternoon?"

His tone was casual, but Cooper could tell he was only pretending not to care. She knew that despite their argument that afternoon he really wanted their support.

"Uh, tomorrow?" Claire stammered. "We're helping our moms at the shop tomorrow."

Cooper's and Claire's mothers had their own interior design business, Ellis Hughes Interiors, and every now and then when things got particularly busy, the girls would spend a Saturday helping out. They mostly sorted through samples and ran errands. Nothing too exciting, but still it needed to be done, and it paid better than baby-sitting or any of the few other jobs they were qualified for at not yet sixteen.

"Whatever," Alex replied with a shrug.

"What about Sunday after church?" Cooper suggested. Even though she didn't agree with Alex about how they should proceed with the reading group, she didn't want him to think she was completely deserting him.

"Can't do it. My grandparents are coming. I'll just work on them tomorrow by myself since I have the time. Anyway, all three of us can't work on my computer at once."

"Well, let us know if there's anything you need us to do," Cooper told him, smiling sympathetically. At least she could offer moral support. Still, she hated to see Alex put all this time into something that she was sure would only end with him being disappointed. After all, who was really going to come to their reading group? But Alex was always dreaming big like that, while Cooper preferred to be much more cautious.

✳   ✳   ✳

The rest of the weekend flew by in a whirl, and Cooper forgot all about the reading group and the signs until Monday in honors English. After sliding into her seat and looking toward the front of the classroom, she noticed a large white sheet of paper with the words *Books rule the world* printed on it in crisp, bold black letters. Underneath, the quote was attributed to the French writer Voltaire, and then in smaller letters it said, *Come see what the big deal is in the second-floor student lounge Thursday at 3:00.*

I guess Alex came up with an advertising campaign, Cooper thought ruefully, struggling with her feelings of loss. There it was, *her* reading group up on the board for all to see *and* come to! It was something she wasn't ready to share, and yet everyone was suddenly invited.

It was just like when she was six. Her mother had made her share her brand-new markers she had bought with her birthday money with the little boy next door when he came over to play. It wasn't that Cooper was selfish, she just knew that Eric didn't understand how special the markers were and wouldn't be as careful with them as Cooper was. Her mother told her she was being silly, but Cooper knew she was right. Cooper winced every time Eric ran all the colors together, rubbing the points of the lighter shades in the puddles of dark ink that covered his paper. When he left, Cooper sadly inspected the felt tip under each cap and found them all to be the same ugly shade of brown. They were ruined. She was sure it would be the same with the reading group. It started out as something special, and now all these people who didn't understand that were going to make a big mess of it.

"Hey, do you have an extra pencil?" asked the girl sitting at the next desk, pulling Cooper from her thoughts. Natasha and Cooper had at least one class together each semester and had become in-class friends. Cooper always knew she could count on her for a stick of gum or information on a home-work assignment she forgot to write down, but they never really hung out together outside of school.

"Sure, I know there's one in here somewhere," Cooper replied, rummaging around in her shiny silver backpack. It took her a few minutes to find what she was looking for in her disorganized bag, but when she did, she held the pencil up triumphantly before handing it over.

Natasha took the pencil, then leaned over again. Peering at Cooper from behind a curtain of shiny black hair, she asked, "So what do you suppose is going on in the second-floor lounge this Thursday?"

Without even thinking, Cooper shrugged noncommit-tally, then flipped open her notebook as the final bell rang. Immediately she was stung by her guilty conscience. *Why am I pretending not to know about the reading group?* she asked herself. Well, she didn't actually say she didn't know, she just chose not to answer. As class dragged on, Cooper justified her actions by convincing herself that just because

Alex was all gung ho to promote the reading group didn't mean she had signed up to be a spokesperson. She was under no obligation to invite Natasha. She was under no obligation to invite anyone.

She couldn't escape the subject of the reading group, though. In biology class there was another sign pinned up right under her teacher's favorite poster that featured a close-up of a dissected frog. This time the sign said, *Read, read, read!* with the quote attributed to William Faulkner. Again, at the bottom the meeting time and place were clearly listed.

As Cooper pulled out her textbook, she heard several people discussing the cryptic notes Alex had posted around campus. Thankfully, Mr. Robbins appeared from the back room followed by his teaching assistant, Micah Jacobson, and everyone quieted down.

Micah Jacobson made biology, high school, even life worth living for Cooper. In a manner of speaking, anyway. He was tall and gorgeous and played guitar in one of the only good bands at their school. Cooper knew this last bit of information because on Fridays during lunch, bands made up of Hudson High students gave mini-concerts in the amphitheater, allowing her to hear Micah's band, *Say Aaaah*, several times.

It didn't matter that he had no idea who she was and had never spoken to her directly in the year and a half they had gone to school together. She was sure that someday the gorgeous senior would notice her. Until he did, though, Cooper was content to admire him from a distance. It was much safer anyway, since she had no idea what she'd say to him if and when they did finally speak.

Cooper forgot that this was their first dissection day, and she was so busy daydreaming about Micah she didn't notice the object of her year-long obsession approach her desk until he dropped a stained white lab coat and a pair of scratched plastic goggles in front of her. He was there and then gone so fast that by the time she realized it was him, he had moved on to the next desk in the row and she was left to stare after him wistfully. She hadn't even been able to choke out the word "thanks."

When Micah was done, Mr. Robbins began assigning lab partners. As soon as Cooper heard her name read, she reluctantly made her way to her assigned lab station, forgetting to pay attention to who her partner would be. Once there, she busied herself putting on her lab coat and slipping her goggles around her neck, where they hung like a big, unstylish necklace.

Isn't it bad enough that the only time I get to spend with Micah is in a gross lab with the smell of formaldehyde clinging to my hair and clothes? Cooper thought. *Now I have to dress up like a mad scientist, too. The things I'm forced to do in the name of education!* She sighed.

"Here, I picked up our worm," someone behind her announced, placing a preservative-soaked earthworm into the crusty-looking dissecting tray that had been left at their station.

"*Our* worm?" Cooper questioned, spinning around to see who the deep male voice belonged to. It was Josh Something-or-other. They'd had a class together freshman year, but Cooper couldn't remember which one. Still, she could've done worse as far as lab partners went. She knew enough of him to be relatively sure he wasn't one of those obnoxious, immature guys who would try to make her scream by flinging worm guts at her or anything.

"Yes, *our* worm," he repeated, breaking into Cooper's

27

thoughts. "Unless, of course, you'd like it to be *your* worm. In that case, I'd be perfectly happy to sit back and watch while you dissect him."

"Weren't you paying attention in class yesterday?" Cooper asked. "Worms are asexual, so it can't be a him."

"Oh, excuse me! I'd be perfectly happy to sit back and watch while you dissect *it*, then."

"That's really not necessary," Cooper shot back, beginning to backpedal. "It's nice of you to offer, but I don't want to hog all the fun. You go right ahead and think of it as *our* worm. Really, I insist."

"Thanks," he said wryly while Cooper continued to search her memory bank for his last name.

Finally she glanced down at the countertop and saw a red notebook with "Josh Trobisch" printed in the upper right-hand corner. He had nice writing for a guy. *Good, that means I won't be responsible for writing up all our joint lab assignments like I usually am when I get paired with a guy.*

Just as Cooper was getting into the rhythm of their banter, Josh turned his attention to his textbook. Not really having anything important to say, she flipped her book open, too, and studied the diagram of what she could expect to find inside her worm. Correction: *their* worm. She read for several minutes before deciding she might as well go ahead and pin the ugly creature down. Just as Cooper reached for the tweezers, Josh did, too. She jumped when their hands accidentally collided, sending the tweezers, the dissecting tray, and the worm crashing to the ground—and causing everyone in the class to turn away from their own projects to see what was going on.

"You need some help over there?" Micah called from the

front of the room while Cooper tried to will her cheeks not to turn bright pink.

I can't believe it! The first time he ever speaks to me, and it's because I dropped a worm! I am so clumsy! Cooper silently chided herself. She was still agonizing over the embarrassing incident when her lab partner answered Micah's question for her.

"Everything's under control," Josh replied. "Our worm was trying to make a run for it, but we've got him—I mean *it*—subdued," he explained, kindly drawing everyone's attention away from Cooper. She took the opportunity to quickly reach down and retrieve her science project from the laboratory floor.

When their worm and all the various instruments they would use to torture it were once again in their proper places, Cooper tried to apologize to Josh.

"Sorry, I'm such a klutz," she began. "I probably should have warned you up front that I am constantly knocking things over."

"Don't worry about it," Josh replied, dismissing the incident as if it were nothing. "It wasn't entirely your fault," he insisted. "I'm sure if I'd been wearing my protective eyewear like Mr. Robbins told us to, none of this would have happened." A devious smile lit up his face as he explained in a perfect imitation of Mr. Robbins' voice that " 'Failure to use safety gear is the cause of nine out of ten injuries in the lab.' " With that, he snapped his goggles into place, and Cooper couldn't help laughing at how ridiculous he looked.

When the lunch bell rang, Cooper and Josh were nowhere near finished. They had to label their worm before stowing it in the back room until the next day's class.

"How about if we call it Chris?" Josh asked. "You know,

since it's not really a boy or a girl and that name can go either way."

"Sure, whatever," Cooper replied distractedly as Josh began neatly printing the nongender-specific name on a piece of masking tape. She was too concerned about having ruined any chance she might ever have with Micah to pay much attention to what her lab partner was saying. Still, she was aware enough to realize that Josh was doing most of the cleanup. She didn't want him thinking she was a lazy lab partner, especially after he'd been so nice about her little mishap.

"I'll turn in your lab coat and goggles for you, okay?" she suggested, making her way to the front of the room before he could respond. When she got back to their lab station, everything was back in its place, so Cooper headed for the door, extremely relieved that class was finally over.

"Hey! Thanks," Josh called out from behind her.

Cooper waved over her shoulder without turning around as she took the stairs two at a time. She would definitely be the last one to the cafeteria today.

THE LINE AT THE COKE machine was especially long for some reason, and by the time Cooper made her way out to the courtyard, her mood had gone from bad to worse. Apparently this showed on her face because before she said a word, Alex inquired, "Bad day in bio lab, Miss Ellis?"

"The worst, Mr. Morrow," she replied politely, then turning her gaze on both her friends, she queried, "You're familiar with the term 'fashion victim'?"

"What are you talking about? You look fine," Claire decreed loyally after looking Cooper up and down, taking in her black jumper and shiny silver baby tee.

"Sure, I look fine now, but in biology, when it really mattered, I looked like Dr. Jekyll."

"Mr. Robbins pulled out the old lab coats, eh?" Alex asked.

"And that's just the beginning. Then I knocked my worm on the floor, and now Micah, who until today had a completely neutral opinion of me, thinks I'm an idiot," Cooper wailed.

"Just because you dropped a worm?" Alex and Claire said in unison.

"If only that were all, but you know me. Do I ever *just* drop something?"

Understanding began to dawn on Alex's and Claire's faces before Cooper even started to fill them in on the details of the fiasco.

"I'm in awe," Alex told her when she was finished. "It's almost like you have a special talent for knocking things over. Really, I don't know anyone who manages to do it as well as you. I think maybe it's your spiritual gift."

"Joke if you must," Cooper replied melodramatically. "It's just my life we're talking about."

"Oh, Alex, I almost forgot. Great job with the signs," Claire chimed in, effectively changing the subject and putting an end to Cooper and Alex's lighthearted bickering.

"Thanks," Alex said, suddenly becoming more serious. "I thought something basic but a little mysterious was our best bet," he explained. "You know, get people talking."

"Well, it seems to be working," Claire told him. "Everyone in my last two classes was trying to figure them out."

"In my classes, too," Cooper grudgingly admitted.

"Great! It looks like we might actually get some new blood in the reading group, then," Alex enthused.

"I wouldn't get your hopes up too high," Cooper cautioned. "Just because they're interested in the signs doesn't mean they'll want to join the reading group."

"It's a start," Alex pointed out.

"And I thought you were going to come up with a name. What happened?" Cooper asked.

"I did come up with a name: The Reading Group."

Cooper looked at her friend like he was crazy. "You didn't come up with that! That's what we've always called it!" she protested.

"No, we've always called it 'the reading group'—all lowercase. But now it's 'The Reading Group,' you know, with capital letters, making it a proper name," Alex patiently explained, as if Cooper were a small child.

"Claire," Cooper whispered in a conspiratorial tone, "I think Alex with a capital *A* has been sitting a little too close to the television with a lowercase *T*, and it's melted his capital *B* brain."

"Go ahead and laugh," Alex said. "But wait until Thursday and you'll see. It's going to be a whole new reading group."

"That's what I'm afraid of," Cooper said quietly, her smile gone now. "That's what I'm afraid of."

✤   ✤   ✤

After much persuasion, Cooper scored what she felt was a major victory: convincing Alex not to alter the actual format of the reading group. She conceded that if new people came—and she was careful to stress if—it would be important to have a moderator. Cooper was all for Alex taking the job, but beyond that, she insisted they should try to keep it as informal as possible. He went along with it after she agreed they could always adjust things later if they needed to.

On Thursday, Cooper, Claire, and Alex were comfortably situated on two of the three overstuffed, decades-old couches that lined the walls of the second-floor student lounge. It was 3:10 and they were the only ones in the room, a fact that prompted conflicting emotions in Cooper. On the one hand, she was elated that their little group might actually stay the same. But at the same time, the hopeful look on

Alex's face made her think that maybe one or two new people might not be such a horrible thing. It would make him so happy, and he had worked so hard on the signs and everything.

Cooper changed her mind a few minutes later when a group of students loudly entered the room. They came to a halt in the middle of the floor, where they proceeded to size up the tiny gathering as if Cooper, Claire, and Alex weren't even there.

In the center of it all stood Jana Schumacher, a girl Cooper knew only well enough to know she didn't want to get any better acquainted. As always, Jana was surrounded by her entourage: Lindsay, who was like a poor-quality Xerox of her popular friend—the smudgy kind that old, beat-up copy machines produce—but with dark hair; and Blake, who sported a pierced eyebrow and bleached blond hair with dark roots—this month, anyway. Anne was the only one Cooper could possibly tolerate. A tall, quiet girl with straight brown hair parted down the middle, she'd been in some of Cooper's classes. When she wasn't around Jana, she was actually pretty nice to talk to. Also, she was intimidatingly smart but didn't flaunt it.

This was worse than Cooper had imagined, and she gave Claire a what-are-we-going-to-do-now look. At almost the same moment, Alex got up off the cushy blue couch he was sitting on and stepped forward to welcome Jana and her friends.

"Hi," Jana responded, tossing her long blond hair over her shoulder and smiling a little too sweetly. "Are we late?"

"No, not at all," Alex told them, then motioned to an empty couch covered in a worn red velvety fabric.

"Okay, we're ready to go, so let's crack open those books.

What are we reading?" Jana cheerfully queried while her three friends remained silent. They seemed very used to sitting back and letting her do the talking. Cooper couldn't help thinking that Jana's interest in the reading group seemed a little forced.

"Uh, we're reading *The Screwtape Letters* by C. S. Lewis," Alex replied, stammering a bit after being caught off guard by Jana's enthusiasm. It took him only a minute to regain his composure. "Before we get started, why don't you tell us a little bit about your interest in the group," Alex suggested, gently steering the conversation.

"Oh sure. We just thought it might be nice to get involved in something, and Mr. Danenhauer told us about your reading group . . . so here we are," Jana explained coolly.

It didn't seem like much of an explanation to Cooper, but it was enough for Alex.

"Well, that's great. We're really glad you came," he welcomed, enthusiastically enough for Claire and Cooper, too.

While everyone waited, Alex pulled a stack of manila folders from his backpack and began passing them out. Cooper knew Alex was planning on putting together some information for any newcomers they might have, but when she peered inside her folder and began thumbing through the contents, she was genuinely surprised to find several different commentaries on *The Screwtape Letters*, as well as a copy of part of the actual book, a biography of C. S. Lewis he'd found on the internet, and three different essays by Lewis "experts" on the author's writing.

That's Alex for you, Cooper thought. *Always over-prepared.*

"I hope you're not overwhelmed by the amount of information I'm giving you," Alex told the group, seeming to read

Cooper's mind. "I just thought a little background information might be nice, and since those of you who are new wouldn't have had a chance to get a copy of the book we're reading yet, I went ahead and made copies of the section we're covering this week so you can follow the discussion."

"No, this is great," Anne told him, seeming genuinely interested. "It's always nice to know the context of what you're reading."

Alex beamed under the new group member's praise. It seemed to be all the encouragement he needed to jump right in. "Well, let's get started, then. Have any of you ever read anything else by C. S. Lewis? Maybe some of the CHRONICLES OF NARNIA books when you were younger?"

The discussion flowed for the entire ninety minutes. Alex had shown Claire and Cooper his plan at lunch, and it included generally discussing Lewis's life and career, then his NARNIA children's books, and finally, after touching on the topic of allegory, they would get to the day's selected reading.

Right from the start, though, Jana seemed intent on derailing the discussion. She kept making negative remarks like, "This isn't a book, it's just a bunch of letters!" and, "What kind of a name is Wormwood?" Even after Alex had explained several times that while *The Screwtape Letters* may look like a simple series of letters from the demon Screwtape to his depraved nephew Wormwood, it was really much more, Jana remained skeptical.

"You see, Jana, this book is Lewis's strong warning against the evil we allow to creep into our lives and slowly poison us," Alex patiently explained, still set on convincing her. "But if Lewis had just written a book telling us all to stop being so selfish and mean to one another, no one would have read it."

The others in the group seemed to get it, but Jana was still hung up on the book's deceptively simple format. Or maybe she just preferred to argue over whether C. S. Lewis was a good writer rather than do any reading. This was exactly the kind of thing Cooper was afraid would happen if they opened up the group.

"I still think it looks easy to write. It's not as if it's Shakespeare or something," Jana continued, causing Cooper to literally bite down on her tongue to keep from rushing to the beloved Christian writer's defense.

"If that's true, then that only proves how good of a writer he really was because all the great writers make it look easy," Alex explained further, not seeming the least bit exasperated.

When Jana still didn't appear to be won over by Alex, Cooper lost it. "Well, if you're convinced it's so 'easy,' why don't you give it a try?" she challenged, sounding just a bit nastier than she had meant to.

"Cooper!" Claire whispered disapprovingly before giving her friend a look that let her know she had crossed the line of politeness, but Alex's face just lit up.

"That's a great idea," he agreed, unable to contain his enthusiasm. "Why don't we each try to write one of Wormwood's letters to Screwtape for next week? That's a perfect solution!"

"Oh great!" Cooper groaned.

"You mean as a homework assignment?" Jana asked, wrinkling her nose in disapproval.

When he nodded in the affirmative, both girls protested loudly, agreeing on a subject for the first and possibly last time.

"Just give it a try," Alex coaxed, and surprisingly Jana acquiesced.

"Well, since *you* asked me to," she replied, looking innocently at Alex despite her obvious meaning.

Ooooh! Cooper seethed, willing herself not to respond. *She's just doing that on purpose to make it look like I'm the one being difficult. Well, I won't let her get away with it!*

"I guess it could be kind of interesting," she told Alex, trying really hard to sound positive. She was sure if he looked closely, though, he would recognize the smile plastered across her face as the fake one she reserved for cheek-pinching relatives. Thankfully, he didn't look closely.

"Great! Then I guess that's it for today," Alex said. "I hope to see you all back here next week. Remember, the reading for next week is on the schedule in your folder. I've also listed a few bookstores that I know have several copies of the book in stock for those of you who don't have it yet."

As Jana and her friends streamed out of the lounge, Cooper had to admit to herself that the group hadn't gone any worse than she had feared it would. Of course, that wasn't saying too much, since she had expected it to be a total disaster.

IN BIOLOGY CLASS the next day, Cooper was relieved to see a black TV cart parked at the front of the room near Mr. Robbins' desk.

Good. No dissecting today, she thought with a smile.

"Can you believe it? It's a Friday *and* we get a video!" Josh leaned across the aisle as soon as Cooper was seated.

"Oh, I almost forgot it was Friday," Cooper replied tiredly before tucking her hair neatly behind her ears for the millionth time that day. "I thought this week was never going to end."

"I know what you mean, but hang in there. Just two more classes to go and we're free," Josh reminded her.

"Two more classes like this, and I just might make it," Cooper smiled, glancing at the VCR again. "Actually, as long as I'm not asked to cut anything open, I think I can get through the rest of today just fine, and there's not much chance of that in geometry or gym."

"Yeah, I think you're safe," Josh agreed. "There's not really any point dissecting an isosceles triangle or a basketball."

Before Cooper could respond, Micah appeared out of nowhere and began setting up the video that would occupy the class for the next forty-five minutes. Her train of thought was completely derailed at the sight of him. It took Josh waving his hand in front of her face to bring her back to earth.

"Huh? I'm sorry. Uh, what did you say?" Cooper absently asked, slowly returning to reality.

"Nothing," Josh shrugged, a look of confusion on his face as he attempted to follow her line of vision to figure out what she found so interesting at the front of the room.

Cooper panicked when she realized what he was doing. That was all she needed, Josh figuring out that she had a gigantic crush on a senior who didn't even know she existed. How embarrassing would that be? She quickly tried to resume their conversation and turn his attention away from the VCR cart and Micah.

"So . . . any big plans this weekend?" she asked, forcing herself not to let her eyes dart to the front of the classroom even for a second.

Josh's look of confusion turned to one of pleasant surprise. He seemed genuinely pleased that she was interested. "Actually, there's an all-ages show at a club downtown that I'm going to with some friends tomorrow night."

Now it was Cooper's turn to be surprised. She hadn't pegged Josh as a "club kid." The whole thing was rumored to be a huge drug scene, and Cooper had never really understood the attraction. Still, she felt she should at least respond, but when she opened her mouth all that escaped was a small "oh."

"What?" Josh queried, picking up on her obvious lack of enthusiasm.

"I'm not really into the club scene," she explained, trying hard to keep the tone of disapproval out of her voice.

"No, it's not that kind of club!" he responded, smiling at

her confusion. "I'm not, like, hanging out at Limelight or something," he told her, naming one of the more notorious clubs known for its wild parties.

"You said a club," Cooper replied a little defensively.

"It's just a music club in Greenwich Village, and there's an all-ages show. Don't you ever go to concerts or anything?" Josh continued.

"Not that often," Cooper explained, wishing the video would hurry up and start already.

"Well, to be honest, I don't, either," Josh explained, seeming a little embarrassed. "But my older brother goes to Georgetown, you know, in Washington, D.C., and he started going to hear this local band called *Eddie From Ohio* a lot. He brought their CDs home over Christmas break, and they're all I heard for two weeks, but I had to admit they were really good. Kind of alternative-folk or something, and they come up to New York every other month or so for a show. Anyway, my brother convinced me I had to go see them live . . . so I'm going. You should come."

"Oh, I don't think so," Cooper told him, shaking her head at the same time as if to really make her point.

"Don't worry, it won't be wild or anything. They're just really cool," Josh coaxed.

"I can't," Cooper told him. "Claire and I promised Alex we'd go to see some old Alfred Hitchcock movie with him that's playing this weekend only. *Vertigo* or something. I don't know."

"Well, maybe you can make it next time. Claire and Alex can come, too."

"Yeah, maybe," Cooper noncommittally replied. She doubted they'd ever really go. They were a tight-knit trio and kept pretty much to themselves.

Before Josh could say any more, Micah turned out the lights and the video began to roll. It was some program that couldn't have been filmed much later than the 1950s. In fact, Cooper was surprised it was even in color.

"The locust goes through many different life stages," an announcer began in a dull monotone. That sentence alone was enough to let Cooper know she could tune out for the rest of the period. She felt a little guilty as she did, but how could Mr. Robbins really have thought anyone would learn anything from something like that? Besides, now that the classroom was dark, she felt it was safe to watch Micah again without fear of being discovered. So she happily did just that, squinting in the dark until the bell rang and she began her daily sprint to the Coke machine.

❋　　❋　　❋

"So you're saying your lab partner asked you out?" Claire queried over lunch, raising an eyebrow at this new development.

"No!" an appalled Cooper loudly denied, looking around to see if perhaps Claire's question was really meant for someone else. "What are you talking about? Weren't you listening to me?"

"You said he asked you to go hear some band with him, didn't you?"

"That is *so* not the same thing as asking me out," Cooper exasperatedly explained. "Besides, he's going with a group of friends, so I know he didn't mean it like that. The point of my story was that Josh caught me drooling over Micah, not that Josh asked me out. Which, just for the record, he didn't."

"Whatever you say, Cooper. Whatever you say," Claire

repeated in a soothing tone that made it seem more like she was trying to calm a petulant two-year-old than reassure her long-time friend.

Before Cooper could protest, though, Alex gleefully announced, "Oh look, there's Cooper's new boyfriend now!" pointing toward Josh, who was making his way across the cafeteria balancing a tray filled with the school's hot lunch and three cartons of milk.

"Very funny," Cooper shot back, rolling her eyes at her friend. "Why don't you just pass him a note in study hall telling him I like him, too?" she sarcastically suggested.

"Why, I'd be more than happy to," Alex offered, still grinning. "In fact, I'd say it's my duty as a friend, wouldn't you, Claire?"

Claire wisely held her tongue, adopting a Switzerland-like neutrality.

When no one responded, Alex continued to torture Cooper. "You know, he and I have sixth period together. It would be no trouble to, say, let him know you changed your mind, and we'd be happy to join him tomorrow night."

"Don't even think about it," Cooper warned, trying to infuse her voice with all the sternness she could manage, but her effort was wasted. It didn't seem to have any effect on Alex unless it was to just encourage him even more.

"Actually, there's no time like the present," Alex announced, rising from his spot on the courtyard bench.

Cooper was trying to get him to sit back down without making a huge scene. She hissed his name several times under her breath before realizing he was beyond being stopped. Instead, she and Claire watched in amazement and horror as Alex strode across the courtyard toward Josh.

"I'm sorry," Claire said, giving Cooper a sympathetic

look. "Still, it could be worse. I didn't want to say this with Alex around, but Josh *is* really cute. Are you sure you're not even the tiniest bit interested?" she gently asked.

At that, Cooper focused in on Josh. She did have to grudgingly admit that he was pretty cute, with watery-blue eyes, layered light brown hair long enough to tuck behind his ears, and a few pale freckles scattered across his cheeks. And most important, by the way he towered over most of his friends, she knew he had to be at least a few inches taller than she was. Why hadn't she noticed any of that before?

"It doesn't matter if he's cute or not," Cooper explained matter-of-factly, "because he wasn't asking me out. Besides, I'm only interested in Micah."

"Oh yeah," Claire replied flatly.

Cooper knew from past conversations that Claire wasn't exactly Micah's biggest fan. In fact, she thought he was a little stuck-up, but before Cooper could rush to her crush's defense one more time, Alex approached Josh, and Cooper covered her eyes. She was peeking through her fingers, not wanting to watch but unable to resist when Claire began tugging on her hand.

"Put your hands down and try to act natural," she coached. "You don't want him to look over here and see you hiding your eyes, do you?"

At that, Cooper put her hands at her sides and straightened up. Claire was right. And maybe Josh wouldn't believe Alex anyway. She turned her gaze on Claire and tried to forget that Alex was ruining her life. Instead, she asked her friend about her progress on the jacket she was making for her.

Claire had been sewing her own clothes—and some of Cooper's—since she was eleven, and she planned to stay in

New York and study fashion design after they graduated. Cooper loved Claire's stuff and couldn't wait until the day they could go into a store and see it hanging on the rack, although the Claire originals she had hanging in her own closet now were great, too.

"Cupid" finally returned, grinning from ear to ear.

"Don't even talk to me," a disgusted Cooper told him.

"That was a pretty rotten thing to do, Alex," Claire agreed.

"But don't you want to know what he said?" Alex asked.

Cooper said "no" and Claire said "yes" at exactly the same time.

"Well, which is it?"

"Oh, go ahead and tell me so I can assess the damage," Cooper conceded.

"He said . . . Wait! Are you sure you want to know?"

"Al-ex!" both girls practically screamed.

"All right, all right! He said that we were supposed to read chapter five and answer the odd-numbered questions," Alex related while a triumphant smile spread across his smug face.

"You are such a dork sometimes," Cooper told him, pelting him with pretzel sticks.

Just as Cooper was beginning to relax again and Claire returned to her progress report on the jacket, Jana and company plopped down on the bench next to Alex without even waiting to be invited.

"Hey, reading group!" she said cheerfully.

"Hi," each member of the trio replied.

"I just wanted you to know we got our books," Jana reported to Alex.

"That's great. What do you think so far?" he asked.

"I think I understand it a little bit better now, but it's still a bit hard to follow in some places," she admitted.

"You'll get the hang of it," Alex encouraged.

"Yeah, I'm sure I will. If not, you can explain it to me," Jana told him with a smile.

"So are you guys going to that party at Jane's tonight?" Jana asked, even though Cooper was pretty sure she already knew the answer. They never went to parties and Jana always did, so she must have noticed they were never there. Or maybe not. She hadn't really noticed them at all until a few days ago, but now she seemed to be making up for lost time.

"No, it's theme video night at Cooper's every Friday," Alex told her, then went on to explain what that meant.

"That's really neat. My dad's a producer and a huge film buff. He must have at least three hundred videos in his collection, but most of them are kind of obscure."

"Like what?" Alex asked, his interest definitely piqued.

"Oh, I don't know," Jana replied absently. "You'll just have to come over and look through them sometime. I'm sure he'd let you borrow whatever you wanted."

"That'd be great," Alex enthused. "And you're welcome to join us any Friday night when you don't have other plans," he added.

Claire's and Cooper's heads snapped around to stare at him in disbelief.

But none of us ever invites anyone else to video night! Cooper silently screamed. *Especially Alex! It's sacred. At least it used to be. Like the reading group. Like lunch with just the three of us. Like everything lately*, Cooper concluded with a sigh of resignation.

When Jana cheerfully accepted for that night explaining that "Jane's parties are never that great anyway. Her parents always stick around—as if we need a baby-sitter," Cooper didn't even flinch.

VIDEO NIGHT WAS DEFINITELY not the same. Jana brought only Blake with her, but it still changed everything. Cooper uncomfortably offered them something to drink and took their coats before showing them into her family's stark, modern living room.

Claire had brought along the jacket she was making for Cooper to make sure the sleeves were okay. It was short and black, almost like a jean jacket but made from a more light-weight material. It had thick gray stitching around the collar and cuffs, giving it a retro 1940s look that Cooper loved. She couldn't wait until it was done. She planned to wear it with a vintage floral dress she and Claire had found downtown. It wasn't until Jana said "Uh, nice jacket" in a way that let everyone know she really meant exactly the opposite that Cooper realized she had answered the door wearing the unfinished garment.

"Oh! I forgot I had it on," she explained, annoyed at her absentmindedness and at Jana's obvious talent for making her feel stupid. "It's one of Claire's creations, but it's not quite done," she added as she carefully slipped out of the pin-filled jacket.

"You sew?" Jana asked Claire, suddenly full of interest.

"Yes," Claire answered simply, not really one to talk about herself. Cooper had no problem pointing out her friend's talent, though.

"She makes almost all of her own clothes," Cooper volunteered proudly. "In fact, she made that skirt she has on and that top."

"Really?" Jana asked Claire, sounding genuinely impressed. "Maybe you can help me, then. I'm going to this wedding in two weeks with my parents, and I can't find anything to wear. Do you think maybe you could make me something?" she proposed, then quickly chimed in with, "I'd pay you, of course."

Before Claire could say anything, Jana continued to gush. "It's just that you've got *such* great taste, and I know if you went with me you'd pick out the *perfect* pattern and material. Please, I'm begging you."

She's really laying it on thick, Cooper thought. *And how presumptuous to assume Claire will just drop everything to go shopping with her and make her a dress.*

"Sure, I guess I could," Claire agreed much to Cooper's amazement. But then, that was just like Claire to be so nice.

"Great! How about we go shopping tomorrow? I want to give you plenty of time to work on it. I'll even treat you to lunch. What do you say?"

Claire looked helplessly at Cooper before hesitantly agreeing. The girls had talked about Rollerblading in Central Park in the afternoon, but nothing was set in stone. Still, it annoyed Cooper that Claire so easily blew off their tentative plans.

"You might want to bring Cooper along, too," Claire suggested a few minutes later. "She's great with accessories and always manages to find the perfect necklace or earrings when I never can."

"Oh . . . uh, sure," Jana stammered. "Cooper's welcome to come." But by the way she said it and the way she didn't even issue the invitation directly to Cooper, it was obvious she'd just as soon Claire come alone.

Cooper was only too happy to oblige, not wanting to spend the day feeling like the odd shopper out. "I better not. I really have a lot of homework," she explained, which was true. But she could just as easily have done her studying on Sunday.

"I guess it will just be the two of us, then," Jana cheerily said.

"I guess so," Claire repeated.

"Now that all the shopping plans are settled, can we finally start the first movie?" a slightly annoyed Alex asked. Everyone agreed, but as soon as Alex announced the evening's theme: popular actors' first movies—"It's sort of my own version of 'Before They Were Stars,' " he explained— Jana began suggesting all the other movies Alex could have chosen and continued to do so all through the first video.

Cooper tried really hard not to spend the evening pouting in the corner, but she couldn't help feeling left out.

Jana has her own perfectly good friends. Why does she have to try to steal mine away? Cooper wondered a little self-pityingly as she stared blankly at the large television screen. It's not that she envied the attention Jana was giving to Claire and Alex. She didn't even like Jana. It just hurt to see her friends being pulled away from her and sucked in by this outsider's obviously fake charm.

At the end of the night she still didn't feel any better. She said good-bye to her friends and Jana and Blake, then shuffled back into the living room dejectedly. There she settled back in front of the TV, this time watching reruns of *Mary Tyler Moore* and *I Dream of Jeannie* on Nick at Nite. It was after 1:00 when her dad came out to get some juice and suggested she should probably go to bed. *The Bob Newhart Show* was on now, not a particular favorite, and she groggily hit the power button and padded off to her room after giving her dad a kiss on his whiskery cheek. As tired as she was, though, she spent a fitful night.

❆ ❆ ❆

It was 10:00 when Cooper made her way into the kitchen the next morning, which wasn't unusual. She would stay up late and sleep in every day if she could. She had always hated mornings, unlike her mother, who cheerfully greeted her.

"Good morning, sweetheart. Do you want a muffin or some kiwi? Or there's fresh-squeezed juice in the fridge."

Cooper only grunted as she made her way to the fridge to inspect its contents for herself. She didn't know how her mom always managed to be perfectly put together—not a strand of sable-colored hair out of place—at any time of the day or night when Cooper couldn't even bear to speak until she had been up for at least an hour. Cooper smoothed her own sleep-tangled hair and attempted to straighten her faded men's flannel pajama bottoms and T-shirt as she took in her mom's casual tan suit and coordinated print scarf. That was just another of the many differences between mother and daughter: Cooper would never dress up on a Saturday. School was one thing, but Cooper believed weekends were a jeans-only zone.

When she couldn't find what she was searching for, she

was forced to utter a few words, but not without great effort. "Don't we have any bagels?" she managed to ask, looking in her mom's direction.

"They're in a bag on the counter," Mrs. Ellis said. Then, anticipating her next question, added, "And the cream cheese is behind the juice."

"Thanks," Cooper mumbled as she began digging around in the Ess-a-Bagel bag for a cinnamon-raisin one. They were her favorite and her mom knew that, but it didn't stop Mrs. Ellis from trying to push fruit off on her daughter each morning.

Cooper slumped in a chair with her freshly toasted bagel and pulled one knee up to her chest, using it as a table to hold one half of her breakfast while she quickly devoured the other half. Her mother gave her a disapproving look.

"We have a table for that, you know," Mrs. Ellis pointed out.

Cooper shook her head in acknowledgment of her mother's comment before scooping up the rest of her bagel and taking a big bite. In the process she managed to smear cream cheese on the tip of her nose, which she quickly wiped with the sleeve of her T-shirt. Luckily her mother wasn't looking.

"So what are you and Claire up to today?" her mother innocently asked, unaware of the flood of emotions the question would trigger for Cooper.

"What makes you think I'm doing something with Claire?" Cooper replied, trying hard to sound nonchalant.

"Because you're *always* doing something with Claire or Alex or Claire *and* Alex. I figured I was safe in assuming today would be no different."

"I thought so, too," Cooper admitted, "but Claire is helping some girl from school with a dress, and Alex is sitting in on some boring film seminar at NYU, so it looks like I'm on my own."

"Well, I'm going to Bloomingdale's in a bit. Why don't you come along?" her mother kindly suggested.

"I don't know. I don't really feel like shopping," Cooper answered. It's not that she didn't appreciate the gesture, but Cooper and her mother had very different opinions about how Cooper should dress. The less they shopped together the better as far as she was concerned. Especially in the last year or two, as Cooper developed her own style, their expeditions always seemed to end in a fight.

"Come on, you said the other day you needed a few warmer things for school now that winter's really here, and I'll try to keep my opinions to a minimum. It's better than moping around the apartment all day, looking like you just lost your best friend."

"Okay," Cooper finally agreed. "You're probably right."

"You'd better run and hop in the shower, then," her mom directed, quickly taking control of the situation and the outing. "I want to get going pretty soon."

❅   ❅   ❅

"Cooper, honey, are you sure you don't just want to try a little base? It would really even out your complexion."

They had made it through an hour in the dressing room, and Cooper even had two new pairs of pants and some warm cotton tights to show for it, but the makeup counters were always a battlefield. Mrs. Ellis was always making suggestions that seemed helpful, but to Cooper they sounded like criticisms.

"I didn't know my complexion needed evening out," Cooper replied tensely.

"Don't take everything so personally. All women need a little help," her mom explained.

It wasn't as if Cooper didn't wear makeup, she just preferred a lighter touch than her mother on most days. But she also liked experimenting occasionally with the wild colors she and Claire would pick up from the little shops down in SoHo and Greenwich Village. Mrs. Ellis would have liked Cooper to settle somewhere in between.

"How about some nail polish?" her mom suggested, not giving up easily. "Anything would be better than that horrid silver stuff you're wearing."

"I guess I could use a sort of rosy brown," Cooper agreed, inspecting her shiny, metallic-looking nails. She appreciated her mother's willingness to spend money on her, she just wished her mother would keep her mouth closed in the process.

"Wonderful! I know just the place," Mrs. Ellis said, quickly steering Cooper past several counters and over to a display of Chanel nail colors.

Cooper was busy painting one stripe of each color she was considering across a different nail when a tall, dark-skinned woman with her hair pulled into a sleek bun approached her. At first Cooper thought maybe she was a saleswoman, but she wasn't wearing a name tag and she had a large black bag slung over her shoulder.

"Excuse me, but can I ask you if you're with an agency?" the woman inquired cryptically.

"What?" Cooper answered, looking down the length of the counter to where her mom was busily sampling some skin-care products.

"Are you with a modeling agency?" the woman asked. "I guess not since you had no idea what I was talking about."

"Uh, no, I'm not," Cooper agreed.

"You must get asked that all the time, though, with your height and your striking features," the mystery woman continued.

"Sometimes," Cooper admitted, then sheepishly added, "but most of the time it's by creepy guys on the subway trying to pick me up."

"Well, I'm surprised to hear that."

"Oh" was all Cooper could think to answer. That seemed to jolt the woman into action.

"I'm sorry! You must think I'm so rude, interrogating you at the cosmetics counter like this without even introducing myself! My name is Tara Jefferson. I'm with Yakomina Models," the woman finally explained just as Mrs. Ellis returned to Cooper's side.

"Did you find something, honey?" Mrs. Ellis absently asked before noticing she and her daughter weren't alone.

"Yeah, but, Mom, this is Tara Jefferson with . . . um, I'm sorry, what did you say again?" Cooper tried to explain.

"Yakomina Models," Tara repeated.

"And I'm Louise Ellis," Mrs. Ellis said, offering a hand to the stranger.

"I was just asking your daughter if she'd ever done any modeling," Tara explained.

"Really?" Mrs. Ellis questioned, her eyes wide. "You know, I tried to get her to take some modeling classes a few years back, but she just refused. She's a little sensitive about her height."

"Well, compared to some of the models I work with, you're not that tall at all," Tara told Cooper, smiling kindly.

"Tell that to the kids at school," Cooper instructed. "I get so tired of being asked why I'm not on the basketball team."

"Maybe it's time you let your height work for you, then," Tara suggested.

"You're not saying you think she could be a model?" a disbelieving Mrs. Ellis asked.

"I'd like to find out," Tara replied. "If you're interested, that is," she told Cooper.

"Of course she's interested," Mrs. Ellis answered for her. "This is a great opportunity."

"I'm not sure," Cooper quietly chimed in. "I don't know if I could really do it. All those women in magazines look so perfect."

"They get a bit of help," Tara confided.

"That's what I was just telling her!" Mrs. Ellis triumphantly declared. "Every woman needs a little help."

Tara only nodded politely. "Look, I don't want to push you into anything you don't want to do, and I'm not promising we'd even sign you if you were interested. Why don't you take my card and think about it for a few days. Talk it over with your mother, and if you'd like to hear more, you can give me a call and we'll set up an appointment."

"Thanks," Cooper said, reaching for the card at the same time her mother did. "It was nice meeting you."

"You'll be hearing from us," Mrs. Ellis assured Tara as she turned to leave.

AT THE MOVIE that night Cooper didn't mention anything
about meeting Tara to Claire and Alex. Her mom talked about
nothing else the entire afternoon and already the subject was
getting old. It was just nice for them to be together without
Jana intruding, to have a normal night out with her friends.

At Claire's after the movie, Cooper got to see the pattern
and material for Jana's dress. The girls had chosen sapphire
blue velvet with chiffon in the same color for the dress's
transparent sleeves. The dress itself wasn't something Cooper would ever wear, but she knew it would be pretty. Also,
lying on Claire's bed was a new backpack.

"Where'd you finally find it?" Cooper excitedly asked,
picking it up. She and Claire had been looking for the black
rubber packs made from recycled tire tubes and old seat belts
ever since they saw them in a magazine a few months earlier.
Each one also had a real license plate stuck to the flap, but
of course they were only the tiny kind issued for motorcy-
cles. Claire and Cooper had been searching in vain to find
bags with New York plates. All the ones they ever saw were
Kentucky or Georgia, and they agreed that just wouldn't do.

"They were at Canal Jeans," Claire explained and then, as

if embarrassed, added, "Jana bought it for me for making the dress."

"Oh, well, that was nice of her," Cooper managed to say without much feeling.

"Maybe we can go down there sometime this week after school and get you one, too," Claire offered.

"Yeah, maybe," Cooper halfheartedly agreed.

❊   ❊   ❊

School on Monday was even worse. After waiting in the miles-long Coke-machine line, Cooper emerged from the cafeteria only to find that Jana and her friends had joined them . . . again. As she got closer she noticed that Jana had a backpack just like Claire's new one, and she was handing a stack of videos to Alex.

"I wasn't sure what you'd want, but the labels on these say they have actual outtakes, and I thought that might be cool," Jana explained, "since it's stuff you can't get at the video store."

"You were right!" Alex told her, giving her an enthusiastic hug. "And they were talking about this film at the seminar I went to over the weekend!" he added after reading the labels for himself.

"That wasn't that film thingie at NYU, was it?" Jana queried.

"Yeah, it was great," Alex replied. "They had screenwriters and directors and even producers there all telling these great stories."

"I think my dad was speaking at that," Jana mentioned casually.

"I don't remember hearing a Schumacher," Alex told her

after seeming to run down some sort of mental participation list in his mind.

"That's because he doesn't use his real name. Did you hear a Paul Yates? If you did, that's my dad. He uses his mom's maiden name so we don't get people showing up on our doorstep with scripts or movie ideas in the middle of the night. You'd be amazed how many weirdoes are out there."

"Paul Yates is your dad?" an incredulous Alex asked. "I heard him speak for two hours the other day!"

"That's nothing. You should hear him when he starts lecturing me about cleaning my room. That can last for three or four hours," Jana joked.

"No, I mean he's great!" Alex clarified. "I was hanging on his every word. He's produced some great independent films."

"I think most of them are just strange," Jana confided. "I don't know why he can't just do normal stuff. Something that Winona Ryder or Brad Pitt might want to be in would be a nice change."

"No, no, no," Alex protested. "You're missing the point. Everyone's doing normal stuff. The stuff he does is much, much better," he explained, trying to convince Jana of what he so strongly believed.

"Whatever," she replied dismissively, obviously eager to change the subject to something she had a little more control over, or at least an interest in.

"Claire and I saw the absolute cutest guy in the entire world on Saturday, and I am completely in love!" Jana announced, then launched into a wild tale of their lunch at The Cupping Room, a little cafe on trendy West Broadway.

"He was the maître d' or the manager or something, wasn't he, Claire?" Jana asked. When Claire simply nodded,

Jana quickly jumped back into her story. "Anyway, he was so gorgeous—Italian, I think, but maybe Spanish—with dark hair and these great eyes, and I couldn't stop staring at him long enough to take even one bite of the omelet I ordered. I knew I was going to have to talk to him or I would just die. So we're sitting there, and I'm just completely melting when all of a sudden this girl walks in. No big deal. She was wearing black leggings and an oversized denim shirt. Her hair's just pulled back with a clip and she doesn't have a drop of makeup on her face or anything. And just when I thought he was going to show her to a table, he leans over and kisses her! I mean *really* kisses her," Jana said with great emphasis and a raised eyebrow. "I couldn't believe it! My heart broke in a million pieces on the spot."

"I'm sure it was his girlfriend," Claire explained. "They obviously knew each other."

"I don't care. I refuse to give up," Jana said. "I'm still determined to at least talk to him."

"Maybe if you wanted to ask him for directions to the rest room or something, okay—but I don't know about much beyond that," Claire suggested. "I think he's a lot older than you, and he and that girl looked pretty serious."

"We'll see" was all Jana said in reply.

※　　　※　　　※

Tuesday was more of the same. Jana invited Alex over to look through the rest of her dad's video collection and was working on getting him to stay for dinner. She was also trying to convince Claire to venture down to The Cupping Room with her one more time. Cooper, on the other hand, failed to register on Jana's social radar.

By that afternoon Cooper was feeling really depressed. If things continued on like this, she'd be friendless by summertime. The thought of all those muggy New York summer days spent by herself were more than she could take. She needed to find something to occupy her time.

Digging through the piles of clothes, books, and other objects that permanently resided on the desk in her bedroom, she found Tara's card. Swallowing hard, she pulled the phone out from under yesterday's wardrobe and dialed the number before she could chicken out. Five minutes later she and her mother had an appointment set up for the next afternoon.

❋   ❋   ❋

"I still think you might have worn something a little dressier," Mrs. Ellis said, picking tiny pieces of lint from Cooper's fitted denim shirt that she had paired with her black low-slung pants, which she loved.

"I wanted to feel comfortable," Cooper attempted to explain as the elevator carried them to the tenth floor. "I'm nervous enough."

The Yakomina offices weren't what Cooper expected, although she wasn't sure what she thought a modeling agency ought to look like. Emerging from the nondescript Manhattan office building's elevator, Cooper and her mother wandered down a long hallway before they came upon an equally nondescript door that identified the agency only in the smallest, plainest lettering possible—as if maybe they didn't want people to find them. There was a small reception area inside with uncomfortable waiting-room chairs and stacks of magazines piled on the glass coffee table in front of them.

"I have a 4:00 appointment with Tara Jefferson," Cooper announced to the receptionist, who didn't appear overly impressed. She merely motioned to the chairs, then returned her attention to whatever she'd been doing before Cooper and her mother had arrived.

As Cooper went to plop down into the seat next to the one her mother had taken, she hit her shin on the edge of the coffee table.

"Ouch!" she loudly whispered.

"Be careful," her mother admonished too late to do Cooper any good.

"It's a good thing I wore pants, huh?" she asked. "If I had a skirt on, you'd be able to see the big red mark I no doubt have on my leg right now."

She was still busy rubbing the injured spot when she heard the receptionist say into a speaker phone, "Tara, you've got some people out here waiting for you."

"I've got a quick call to make, then I'll be right out," Tara replied. The receptionist didn't bother to relay this message directly to Cooper.

True to her word, though, Tara kept Cooper and Mrs. Ellis waiting only a few minutes and soon strode down the hallway and into the reception area. Her dark hair was once again pulled back into a sleek bun, and her cocoa-colored skin was flawless. She wore tailored black pants with trendy, thick cuffs at the hem and a crisp white blouse with cuff links at her wrists set with big red glass beads.

"Hi, Cooper. Mrs. Ellis. I'm glad you decided to come in. Why don't you both follow me? We can talk in my office."

They followed Tara into a small office that had pictures taped to three walls and a large dry-erase board on the other. The board had girls' names listed at the top and what Cooper guessed to be appointments underneath. She wondered if soon her name would be on that board and her pictures on those walls. It was hard to imagine.

"Let me start by telling you that if you have any fantasies about modeling being all glamor, I need to smash those right now," Tara began. "It's a lot of hard work, and since you're still in school, it's not likely you're going to shoot to stardom any time in the near future. What we would do is focus on building your portfolio, sending you out on a couple of appointments a week, and then trying to line up a lot of work for you during your school vacations. How does that sound?"

Cooper looked at her mother, then back to Tara. "Fine, I guess," she replied, not sure what she was expected to say.

"Good, then we can move ahead," Tara said in a firm tone. "Now, I see you doing editorial, which means mainly magazines and possibly some work with different designers. The other option is catalog, which is more suited to girl-next-door types. You are so striking—or you could be with a little help—that I don't see you fitting in there. Still, some of the bigger catalogs like Bloomingdale's and Saks Fifth Avenue will use editorial girls because they want a more sophisticated look, so I'm not saying you'll never do catalog work."

Cooper must have looked confused because Tara stopped at that point and asked, "Have I totally lost you?"

"No, we understand," Mrs. Ellis replied. "There's editorial or catalog work, and you think Cooper is best suited to editorial. It's just that sometimes the two overlap," she repeated.

"Exactly!" Tara said. "So if that sounds good to you, I'd like to talk a little about your appearance."

"Wha-what about my appearance?" Cooper stammered, suddenly feeling a little uncomfortable.

"Nothing too painful," Tara reassured her. "I just want to go over a few things like diet and skin care with you. Actually, this book covers most everything, and it's got some great hair and makeup tips in it, too," she explained with a smile before handing Cooper a copy of a thick, hardbound book. Cooper counted five more copies on Tara's shelf.

"Most of it's just common sense," Tara continued. "Get plenty of sleep, drink a lot of water, watch what you eat, and take care of your skin. The same things your mother probably tells you all the time."

"Maybe you can get her to eat more fresh fruit and vegetables," Mrs. Ellis commented, lifting her hands in a gesture of helplessness. "I know I haven't been able to."

"That brings me to my next point. Would you have a problem losing five pounds?" Tara asked matter-of-factly.

"I don't know. I guess not," Cooper replied with a shrug.

"I'm not saying you aren't thin," Tara explained. "It's just that thin in the real world and thin in the modeling world are two different things."

"Of course," Cooper agreed, although she wasn't at all sure she understood what Tara meant. Why did models all have to be abnormally skinny? It seemed unhealthy to her.

"I think that covers just about everything. If I haven't scared you away yet, the next step is to get some test shots done and see how you come across on film. That will tell us a lot. Then, assuming we like what we see, we can talk more about signing you up."

Cooper had a million questions, but she decided that maybe she should wait until after the test shots were done to say any more since they might not even want her after seeing the pictures.

"Oh, I almost forgot!" Tara cried. "Your hair."

"What about my hair?"

"You've got great texture and the color is good, but it could use a little more shape—a few layers would do the trick—and a rinse to brighten it up," Tara rattled off. "I have to tell you that you are incredibly lucky because I was able to line up a cover try for you with a salon magazine. That means they will take care of everything in exchange for putting you on the cover. You'll even get paid a little something for it, and it will give you a taste of what it is like to be in front of the camera before we do your test. What do you think?"

"I think it sounds a little scary," Cooper replied honestly.

"I know, but the makeovers are usually fun, and I think you'll get the hang of things pretty quickly," a confident Tara told her. "Are you willing to give it a try?"

With two pairs of expectant eyes on her, Cooper tried to quickly take her emotional temperature. Did she really want to do this? She couldn't think of any reason not to. Even if Tara ended up not signing her, she'd get a free haircut out of the deal. It might be fun to have people fussing over her, at least for one afternoon.

"Sure," Cooper finally answered, allowing her mother to quit holding her breath in anticipation.

"We want to get moving as quickly as possible," Tara continued. "Is tomorrow after school okay for you?"

"Actually, it isn't," Cooper said. "You see, I have this reading group that meets every Thursday."

"How about Friday, then," Tara suggested, sounding less than thrilled about the scheduling conflict.

"Friday would be great," Cooper agreed while wondering how long it would take and what she'd say to Claire and Alex if she couldn't make it home in time for video night. She still hadn't told them about Yakomina, and she didn't really want to until she was more sure about it. There didn't seem like any reason to if she wasn't going to model. And besides, they were busy with Jana.

"I'll call my contact at the salon magazine, then. I'm sure Friday will be okay for them. Here's the address," Tara said, handing Cooper a business card. "Make sure you're on time."

"Oh, I'll be there and on time," Cooper assured her.

"Great. And in the meantime, I'll try to set someone up to do your test shots Saturday morning. I trust that works for you?'

"That would be fine," Cooper said, although she hoped it wouldn't be too early since it was her only day to really sleep in.

At that, Tara walked Cooper and Mrs. Ellis back out to the reception area.

"I'll call with the details after I set up the test shoot," Tara promised.

Cooper couldn't help wondering if she would hear from Tara after the test shots were done. What if they were a disaster? Would Tara still call and let her know, or would Cooper just be left hanging? She tried to push those thoughts from her mind as she pulled the collar of her coat around her ears and followed her mother out of the building and into a dirty yellow cab with no heater. She'd have her answer soon enough.

"I BROUGHT THAT *Eddie From Ohio* CD I promised to loan you," Josh told Cooper as soon as she arrived in biology on Thursday. He had raved about the show in class on Monday, going on and on about how she had really missed out and trying to get her to promise to come next time. She was still noncommittal, but his offer to loan her his new CD for a day or two to check the band out went above and beyond the call of lab-partner duty, and it was very sweet of him.

"Thanks, I'll bring it back tomorrow," she vowed, carefully stowing the disc in her backpack.

"No rush. You can keep it over the weekend if you want."

"Well . . . thanks. And I promise I really will listen to it," she said, giving him a warm smile. He smiled back self-consciously, and the almost certain interest in his eyes made Cooper blush. Maybe Claire had been right. More than that, Cooper found herself beginning to hope she was.

Cooper was anything but anxious to get to the reading group (or was it The Reading Group?) that afternoon, so when Natasha caught her in the hall and needed some information on an assignment due the next day, Cooper not only told her what she needed to know but stood around chatting about nothing for an additional ten minutes. When she finally did make it to the upstairs lounge, Jana and company were already there.

Cooper's heart sank as she realized that she had actually been hoping against hope that maybe the troublesome girl and her friends would have forgotten all about them and disappeared. She wasn't really surprised that they hadn't, though. What *was* surprising was to find Josh Trobisch sandwiched between Jana and Lindsay.

What is he doing here? Cooper wondered frantically as she squeezed in between Alex and Claire on a couch. *And what is he doing with them?* She knew it had been too good to be true. Josh was so genuinely nice to her, and things were going so well that there had to be a catch. But never in her wildest dreams had she thought Jana would be that catch. She was everywhere!

"So let me tell you what you missed last week," Cooper heard Jana explain. "You see, we're reading a book called *The Screwtape Letters*, which is really just this collection of letters to this demon from his uncle telling him how he can mess up peoples' lives. They're really cool, though."

Even from across the room Cooper could hear everything she said, and she couldn't help noticing how Jana leaned in really close to Josh when she talked to him and touched his arm several times during her explanation. It was obvious they knew each other pretty well.

Cooper tried to focus on the real purpose of the group, on the reading and the spiritual growth she hoped would come from it. It wasn't easy, but she managed through sheer force of will to not obsess over Jana too much that afternoon.

After each of them—with the exception of Josh—shared their version of last week's homework assignment, Alex immediately delved into a new section. Letter eight brought up a huge question that could have been covered for hours, making it somewhat easier for Cooper to get lost in the discussion. The subject was devils and how they came to be seen as comical, harmless creatures with horns sprouting from their heads, who wore red tights and carried pitchforks. In that incarnation it made it almost impossible for any sane person to believe they existed, which Alex pointed out was exactly what Satan wanted. They spent more than an hour wrestling with this issue and rereading Lewis's own beliefs about devils that he spelled out in the book's preface.

" 'Now, if by "the Devil" you mean a power opposite to God and, like God, self-existent from all eternity, the answer is certainly no. There is no uncreated being except God. God has no opposite,' " Alex read.

"But if he doesn't believe in the Devil, why write a whole book about him?" Jana interrupted.

"Hold on, let me finish," Alex implored. "He said he doesn't believe in the Devil, not that he doesn't believe in devils."

"Excuse me! Isn't that the same thing?" she asked.

"No," Alex said. "Listen to what Lewis goes on to say. 'The proper question is whether I believe in devils. I do. That is to say, I believe in angels, and I believe that some of these, by the abuse of their free will, have become enemies of God and, as a corollary, to us. These we may call devils. They do not differ in nature from good angels, but their nature is depraved . . . Satan is the opposite, not of God, but of Michael.' "

"Michael who?" Jana queried.

"Michael is an angel, isn't he?" Josh chimed in, much to the group's surprise.

"Exactly!" Alex answered. "He's sort of a leader among

the angels, actually. In the Bible's book of Daniel, they call him a prince."

"Then does it follow that there are devil princes, too?" Josh asked no one in particular. "That would go along with the point the author was making," he continued. "Satan would be a prince, not a king, because he's Michael's opposite, not God's."

"It makes sense," Alex agreed. "I'm going to ask my pastor on Sunday if he has more info on Michael, though. I have to admit I'm no expert on the subject. I'm just trying to figure it all out, too."

"So now we're going to spend all our time on this?" a disapproving Jana asked. "What about the book?"

"This *is* about the book," Alex explained. "The whole book is about devils. Understanding what we and the author believe about them—and about angels—is necessary to better understand the story."

"Whatever," Jana answered, obviously still miffed.

At that point their time was up. Alex would have to wait for another opportunity to win over Jana.

❊   ❊   ❊

"I think it went pretty well today, don't you guys?" Alex questioned as they made their way down Columbus Avenue. He usually walked with the girls as far as West 72nd Street, where he turned right to catch a #1 or #9 subway train downtown and they turned left toward their apartment building. Alex lived with his father in Chelsea, a younger, eclectic Manhattan neighborhood that Cooper's parents didn't like her wandering around in at night.

"I have to admit having a larger group makes the discussions more interesting," Cooper replied.

"And Josh had some interesting insights, don't you think?" Claire added, nudging Cooper and giving her a knowing look.

"I suppose," Cooper reluctantly agreed. It still bothered her that Josh was so chummy with Jana. And just when she was beginning to allow herself to think about him as possible boyfriend material.

Is there anyone but me who doesn't belong to Jana's inner circle? Cooper silently wondered as they passed the Museum of Natural History. Cooper remembered a field trip she and Claire had taken there with their fourth grade class. *Everything was so much easier then, so predictable.* Cooper sighed. She had always loved museums for that same reason. They were so unchanging, so reliable, showcasing treasures that had been around, unchanged, for hundreds of years. But life wasn't like that.

"Oh, I almost forgot, I have to leave after fifth period tomorrow, so don't wait for me after school. I have a dentist appointment," Claire explained.

"And I'm going to Jana's to look at her dad's video collection," Alex added.

Remembering her own appointment the next day, Cooper was almost thankful to Jana for occupying Alex, at least this one time, so she didn't have to offer an explanation of her own.

"That's fine," Cooper told them. "Are we still on for videos?"

"Always," Alex replied while Claire's head bobbed in agreement.

A few blocks later the girls waved mittened hands at Alex

and shouted their good-byes as he headed in the direction of the Hudson River to the subway station.

Now, if I can only get home from that photo shoot in time, Cooper thought.

8

COOPER RUSHED OUT of the main school building after her final class on Friday, pushing through the throngs of kids that were slowly making their way down the steps. She had twenty minutes to get across town, and she didn't want to upset Tara by being late to her very first appointment. Two blocks south of Hudson High, Cooper was able to hail a cab that cut through Central Park at the 65th Street transverse before speeding south down Lexington Avenue. Even after paying the fare, stopping to check her reflection in a shop window, and making sure the address on the card Tara gave her matched the address painted above the door, Cooper was eight minutes early.

Mrs. Ellis had wanted to accompany Cooper, but luckily she had a design appointment she couldn't rearrange. As nervous as Cooper was, she knew having her mother there would have only added to her anxiety.

With her heart pounding so loudly she was sure it could be heard in Brooklyn, Cooper pushed open the salon door and nervously went inside. She asked for Medea, as she had been instructed, and was quickly escorted into the back. The room looked like its own mini-salon, except for the bright lights surrounding the stylist's chair and camera equipment scattered everywhere.

"So you're our guinea pig for today?" The woman with a British accent seemed to materialize out of nowhere.

"I guess so," Cooper replied, resisting the urge to run from the building.

"Well, I'm Medea and I'm going to be doing your hair," the tall woman explained. "Now, let's take a look at what we've got to work with."

Cooper tried not to squirm as Medea scrutinized her at length, then examined several strands of hair.

"I'd love to go really short," Medea finally announced, and Cooper felt her eyes get large. She hadn't agreed to have all her hair chopped off! What was she going to do? Her panic must have shown on her face because the stylist immediately reassured her.

"Don't worry, we've already decided we're doing long layers on the cover, and we promised Tara we wouldn't cut too much." At that, Cooper was able to relax a little until a photographer entered the room and began setting up even more equipment.

"This is Jean-Paul," Medea said, motioning unnecessarily to the photographer before calling out to him. "Jean-Paul, come meet your subject."

After Cooper shook hands with the photographer, Medea explained that although they planned to use a shot of the finished cut on the cover, they would be taking pictures during the entire process for a feature inside the magazine, as well. With that understood, Cooper was led to a sink to have her hair washed and a conditioning treatment applied.

"Your hair is a little dry, so we're giving it a drink," Medea said as she massaged the creamy goop into Cooper's hair.

When that was done, a makeup artist touched up Cooper's makeup, and the pictures began. There were pictures of her during the coloring process. Still more during the cut, and what seemed like hundreds taken as Medea blow-dried using a huge round brush to coax Cooper's new layers into a smooth, face-framing style.

"See how the brush gave your hair body without making it curl?" Medea pointed out as she ran her fingers through Cooper's shiny hair. "And it's still past your shoulders, so you didn't really lose any length. I just added a bit of shape."

"I really like the color," Cooper admitted. "It looks the same but brighter, just like you said it would."

"Exactly. And now I'm going to add a little glossifier, and then we're all done."

With a final spritz of hair spray, Cooper was finally allowed to get up from the stylist's chair. She wasn't free yet, though. Jean-Paul motioned to a closet and instructed Cooper to change into the clothes hanging from the doorknob without messing up her hair. In the cramped space with rusty pipes lining one wall, Cooper managed to take off her black sweater and slip on the powder-blue top without moving too much. It looked a bit strange with her purple corduroy skirt and black tights, but there wasn't anything else laid out for her to wear. She emerged from the "dressing room" feeling a bit self-conscious.

"That looks fine," Jean-Paul assured her. Cooper was wondering if maybe the photographer was color-blind when he explained that they would just be doing head shots since the hair was the main focus, which meant no one would see anything below her shoulders.

After having her makeup touched up yet again and Medea rearrange a few stray strands of hair, Cooper was posed in a zillion different ways while Jean-Paul shot several roles of film. The hot lights were almost blinding, and just when she thought she couldn't smile even once more or her face would crack, the photographer suddenly announced that he had everything he needed.

Now that she was done, Cooper could finally scratch an itch on her scalp that she had been afraid to deal with during the shoot for fear of ruining her hair. She hadn't wanted Medea to come after her with the hair spray—since she was already wearing enough to keep her hair from moving for the next year. By the time she changed back into her own sweater and retrieved her backpack from the makeshift dressing room, Jean-Paul had already stowed most of his equipment and was busy tearing down the last few lights. Medea was deep in a discussion with the makeup artist, and Cooper didn't know quite what to do. Was she done? Could she just leave? After standing in the middle of the room for several minutes trying to decide, she felt a hand on her shoulder, causing her to flinch reflexively.

"It's just me," Jean-Paul said, laughing at Cooper's jumpiness. "You did a really good job for your first shoot."

"Thank you," Cooper replied, then added, "I hope we'll get a chance to work together again."

"I'm sure we will."

That interchange gave her the confidence to approach Medea and say good-bye, too.

"I just wanted to thank you for my new look," Cooper told the stylist after waiting patiently for a break in the conversation.

"I hope it works out well for you," Medea told her.

"I hope so, too," Cooper replied, remembering the test shots she had scheduled for the morning.

"And don't forget to get yourself a round brush," Medea called after Cooper, who was already heading for the door. "You can find them at the drugstore, but get natural bristles!"

Riding the subway home, Cooper couldn't figure out why she was getting so many strange looks. It took a lot to get people's attention in New York City. She hoped there wasn't something on her face. Only when she casually brushed her cheeks, trying to wipe off any smudges of dirt that might be there, did she figure it out. When she looked down at her hands, her black gloves were covered with pale ivory foundation.

I must look really strange with all this makeup on and my hair sprayed so much it won't even move, Cooper realized with a wave of relief. She was glad to know she hadn't sat in something. After that it was easier to ignore the looks.

Glancing at her watch gave her something new to worry about. Claire and Alex were supposed to be at her house in less than half an hour! At her stop Cooper bolted out of the stuffy subway car and raced up the cement steps to the street. Turning toward home, she sprinted the three blocks to her building and waited impatiently for the elevator, bouncing from foot to foot.

Glancing at her watch again and furiously calculating in her head, she figured she should have just enough time to turn back into the regular Cooper before her friends arrived. She still wasn't ready to tell them about the modeling thing quite yet. She hadn't factored in the time it would take her mother to give her the third degree, though.

"So how did it go?" her mother wanted to know before Cooper was even all the way in the door. "Tell me everything."

Cooper dropped her things in the entryway, then raced

to her bedroom, undressing as she went.

"It went fine!" she called as she threw items of clothing in all directions. After a frantic search, Cooper finally located her favorite pair of faded, baggy overalls and slipped them on over her wrinkled and not completely clean Curious George T-shirt, a Christmas present from Alex. She always teased him about looking like the famous monkey, so he was quite proud of himself when he found the shirt in a shop downtown.

"That's all you have to say?" her mother questioned, appearing in the doorway of Cooper's messy room. She was obviously displeased that her daughter wasn't more forthcoming.

"I don't know," Cooper shrugged, unsure of what her mother wanted to hear. "They were really nice, they did my hair and makeup, and they took a million pictures. That was pretty much it."

"So you think it went well?"

"I hope so, but I don't really know."

Unable to think of anything else to say, Cooper quickly excused herself and rushed down the hall to wash off the thick layer of makeup that was clogging her pores and comb as much hair spray out of her hair as she could. She was almost back to normal when she heard the doorbell ring. Twisting her hair up and fastening it with a large clip, she made her way to the door, bare feet padding against the pale hardwood floor. She felt like herself again.

"I've got it," her mother called before Cooper got there.

By the time she reached the entryway, Claire and Alex were already inside.

"Honey, what did you do to your hair?" Mrs. Ellis asked, looking Cooper up and down. "It looked so pretty when you came home. Didn't you want to show your friends how you looked at your photo shoot?"

Cooper stared in disbelief. She couldn't believe she had forgotten to ask her mother not to say anything. Slapping her hand to her forehead, she sagged against the door in defeat.

"What photo shoot?" Claire and Alex asked in unison.

"You mean you didn't tell them?" Mrs. Ellis asked her daughter, still not catching on. "Why on earth not?"

"It's not a big deal," Cooper insisted, not meeting the eyes of her confused friends.

"I just don't understand you sometimes. It most definitely *is* a big deal. I would think you'd be thrilled, but I guess it's your life. I can't tell you how to feel about things," Mrs. Ellis announced before leaving the room to get ready for her and Mr. Ellis's regular Friday night out.

"So are you going to keep us in suspense or what?" Alex asked impatiently.

"Yeah, why all the mystery?" Claire inquired.

Cooper led them into the kitchen and began her long explanation. Her reasons for keeping quiet made much more sense, though, before she actually said them out loud.

"I just didn't want to make a big deal out of it if they weren't going to sign me. Besides, I wasn't even sure I wanted to do it," she lamely explained.

"Who is this 'they'?" Claire asked.

"And your mom said you already had a photo shoot today . . . so they must have signed you, right?" Alex added.

" 'They' is Yakomina Models," Cooper told them, "and I was just getting a sort-of makeover today. Tomorrow I'm having some test shots done. I have no idea if they're going to offer me a modeling contract or not. I might not know for a couple of weeks."

"Still, I can't believe you didn't say a word about this. We always tell one another everything," Alex reminded.

"I know and I'm sorry. I guess I just felt like you guys were so busy with Jana that you wouldn't care," Cooper admitted.

"That's ridiculous!" Claire said. "We're best friends. One shopping trip with Jana Schumacher won't change that."

"I guess I was just being insecure. You two mean so much to me, I don't know what I'd do without you."

"Lucky for you you'll never have to find out, since you're stuck with us," Alex promised. "I'd say we're the ones who have to worry. Will you still remember us when you're as famous as Claudia Schiffer?"

"Oh please! I'll be lucky if they put me in a Sears catalog."

"I'm sure as soon as they see those pictures, they'll snap you up in a minute," Claire predicted. "You be sure and tell them, though, that you have a standing date for Friday night, so you can't work then."

"It will be the first thing I mention," Cooper promised, holding up two fingers in a boy-scouts-honor vow.

"So can we get to the videos now?" Alex asked, putting one arm around each girl and steering them toward the living room.

"Sure. What's on the menu for tonight?" Cooper inquired.

"Actually, a few videos Jana loaned me this afternoon," Alex replied.

"Oh," Cooper shot back knowingly.

"You're really not giving her a chance," Claire chimed in. "I know she's a little pushy, but she's trying to be nice."

"She's trying to be nice to *you*," Cooper corrected. "She never lowers herself to speak to me."

"Maybe it's because you don't talk to her, either," Claire gently reminded her friend.

"But I tried!" Cooper wailed. "It just seems like from that very first day in the reading group she decided she didn't like me."

"I didn't pick up on that," Alex argued.

"You were too busy running the group, but you guys watch the next time she's around. She will completely ignore me. Just you wait."

"We'll be watching," Claire promised.

"Good," Cooper said, glad that her friends would finally see how horribly Jana treated her. She couldn't believe they hadn't already noticed it.

With that taken care of, the trio settled in for a quiet night of movie-watching. Cooper, remembering Tara's comment about watching what she ate, stuck to snacking on baby carrots and pretzels. To keep her hands busy and her mind off the cookies Alex and Claire were inhaling, Cooper painted her toenails. The midnight blue polish was still drying when the second movie ended, so Cooper had to waddle to the door to see her friends out with cotton stuck between her toes.

"We're on for ice-skating tomorrow, right?" Cooper asked before the pair got into the elevator.

"Of course," Claire answered, but Alex was less enthusiastic.

"I don't know why we can't do something else," he complained. "If God had wanted us to have blades attached to the bottoms of our feet, He would have made us that way."

"Oh, come on! You're getting better," Cooper encouraged. "And besides, this won't be like Rollerblading. We'll be in a rink, so there won't be any awnings or buildings or trees for you to collide with."

"But there will still be people," he pointed out. "*Lots* and *lots* of people."

Cooper couldn't dispute that. In the months following Christmas, Central Park's Wollman Ice Rink was usually packed, but she and Claire loved going there anyway. Alex, on the other hand, only went in exchange for them agreeing to be dragged along to something of his choosing first, and he had picked that Alfred Hitchcock film the previous weekend that the girls attended without complaint. Now it was his turn to compromise.

"I'll be here by 1:00," he finally agreed with much reluctance.

"Good. I should be back from getting my test shots done by then," Cooper said. Tara had called the night before and instructed her to be at the photographer's studio no later than 9:00. Cooper was already tired just thinking of the sleep she was going to miss out on.

"I'll think of you when I get up at noon," Alex teased.

"Go ahead and be a slug if you want. I don't care," she told him as both her friends boarded the elevator, Claire traveling down only a few floors to her family's apartment and Alex heading out into the cold to catch the subway home.

"Be careful," Cooper called out after them, wondering again why Alex wouldn't just take a cab so she didn't have to worry. Her parents and Claire's always insisted that if they were out past nine they had to take a cab home, but since Alex was a boy or maybe because he lived with just his father, no such restrictions were placed on him.

Going back inside her apartment and locking the dead

bolt behind her, Cooper really wanted to watch a little more TV or maybe even read. But Tara had warned her not to show up with dark circles under her eyes, so she knew she better get to bed. She didn't want to look all puffy in the morning.

WHEN THE ALARM WENT OFF at eight, Cooper slammed her open palm against the snooze button, knocking the small clock to the floor before rolling back over and snuggling farther down under the warm blankets. Then somehow, through the fog of sleep, she remembered the test shoot and sat bolt upright in bed. Throwing the covers off and jumping to her feet, she practically ran to the shower, moving faster than she thought she was capable of at that hour of the morning.

Tara had told her to come to the shoot "clean," which she explained meant no makeup and nothing in her hair. Apparently, for some shoots models were asked to come "hair and makeup ready," which meant they had to do their own. But that was usually for catalog work, and to Cooper's great relief Tara had said she most likely wouldn't be doing much of that. This whole modeling thing made her nervous enough without her having to become a makeup artist, too.

Tara had said she could come casual, which was also good since it was too early in the morning to dress up, Cooper concluded. She had slipped on her favorite faded jeans with a thick leather belt and one of her dad's old white dress shirts that she tied in a knot at the waist. Pulling on her heavy black boots and black leather jacket, she raced out the door half an hour later with her hair still wet. Saturday was usually a busy day at her mother's interior design shop, so Mrs. Ellis had left cab fare for her on the entryway table, and Cooper had no trouble flagging one down at that hour.

After telling the driver the address Tara had given her a few days earlier, Cooper leaned back against the hard faux-leather seat of the cab and closed her eyes as Manhattan whizzed by outside the window. They arrived too soon, but the brisk morning air helped wake Cooper up, and since she was twenty minutes early, she decided to grab some coffee. Ducking into a little coffee shop next door to the building where she was to have her photo shoot, she ordered a tall skim mocha latte. After adding three packets of sugar and taking a few tentative sips, she headed next door.

This is it, Cooper thought as she pressed the button for the sixteenth floor and took a deep breath. Staring down at her cardboard coffee cup, she couldn't help wishing that the latte could give courage as well as a caffeine boost. She knew it didn't work that way, though. Instead, she whispered a quiet prayer. *God, please let me do my best . . . and at least not embarrass myself.*

She was surprised when the elevator doors opened not onto a hallway, but to a huge, airy loft. It was a beautiful, sparsely furnished space, and Cooper forgot her nervousness as she took in her surroundings. She wasn't sure how long she was staring at the studio before a voice startled her.

"You must be Cooper," a man in tight black jeans and a white T-shirt said. "I'm Jon."

The camera in his hand was enough for Cooper to identify him as the photographer, and in another corner a makeup artist and hair stylist were set up and waiting. Cooper couldn't come up with a job title for the woman going through a rack of clothes, but she was happy to be able to identify the purpose of most of the people in the room.

"You really lucked out," Jon told Cooper after she had followed him to where he was setting up his cameras. "I did a shoot yesterday for a wonderful new designer, and I still have the clothes. We have some great things to choose from for your shoot."

"That's great," Cooper replied, trying to sound enthusiastic but not fully understanding what was so lucky about it.

"The stylist is picking out some things now, but you better hurry and get your makeup done."

"Oh . . . right," Cooper said, wondering why a stylist was in charge of clothes instead of hair. It was hard to get a feel for the schedule they were on and in what order she was supposed to do things, so she was glad for a little direction. She quickly crossed the light-filled room and settled herself in the makeup chair. It seemed to take forever with all the different bottles, pots, and jars of creams and powders the makeup artist used. Some products were only used for one little thing, Cooper noticed, but she figured they must be important. As a pastel pink cream was dotted under her eyes, she was sure that she had more makeup on that single morning than she had worn in her entire life put together. But when she was done, she couldn't argue with the result. Even with her damp hair hanging around her shoulders, the transformation was amazing. She almost didn't recognize herself, she looked so much older and sophisticated.

The second half of the process focused on Cooper's hair. First it was dried the same way Medea had done the afternoon before, but then it was set on huge Velcro rollers and spritzed with a sweet-smelling styling product. Then, with the rollers still in, she was sent to get dressed.

"Brandi will show you what to put on first," Jon told Cooper when she wandered over to the rack of clothes and stood there, unsure of what to do next.

"Why don't you try this dress?" Brandi, the girl Jon had referred to as the stylist, suggested. It was a short white sleeveless dress with yellow daisies stitched around the neckline and hem. "What size shoe do you wear?" she asked after handing the garment to Cooper.

"I'm usually a nine," Cooper admitted a bit self-consciously. She had always felt a bit embarrassed by her large feet.

Brandi dug through several bags before producing a pair of white sandals with matching daisies on them. "That's not bad for a model. A lot of girls are a nine and a half or ten," she said as she handed over the shoes. Cooper tried but couldn't come up with any sort of appropriate response, so instead, she went to change.

This time there was a larger area to change in, thankfully, although it was separated from the rest of the loft by only a thin white curtain. Just like the previous afternoon, Cooper slipped off her own clothes, careful not to mess up her hair or makeup, and put on what she was given. Surprisingly, the dress fit perfectly. She wondered how Brandi knew.

When she emerged from the dressing room, she returned to the makeup chair and her rollers were removed. The hair stylist had Cooper flip her head upside down and run her fingers through her hair before standing back up. Instead of brushing, her hair was carefully arranged and then sprayed. When she looked in the mirror, she was amazed at the volume that technique had created. It looked totally different from when Medea had done it but just as great in its own way.

"What's that on your toes?" Jon asked when Cooper stood before the camera for the first time.

"Blue nail polish," Cooper admitted a little sheepishly. She hadn't even thought of that the night before when she had painted them. How could she have known they would have her wearing sandals in February?

"Brandi, we need some polish remover," Jon yelled.

"I'm really sorry," Cooper told him as she swabbed the remover across each of her toenails.

"It's no big deal. You didn't know," Jon kindly said. "But in the future, I'd stick with clear or something a little more neutral," he suggested.

"I will," Cooper assured him before smiling gratefully. "I promise."

After the nail polish problem, getting her picture taken turned out to be easier than getting ready to have it taken. Jon was really nice and helped her make up little stories to create the mood he was looking for, like imagining she was standing in a field of wild flowers on a scorching hot summer day or waiting outside a Paris cafe on a rainy Saturday for her boyfriend who she hadn't seen in months. The imaginary boyfriend had Micah's face, so the look of hope and expectation Jon was after came naturally.

Brandi had several other outfits set aside, and Cooper changed three times. One time the shoes that went with a particular outfit were too big and the toes had to be stuffed with cotton, but that was the only hitch and it was minor. With each wardrobe change, her hair and makeup were touched up, too. For the final shots, some tiny clips were added to Cooper's hair, sweeping her long layers to the side.

Her lipstick color was changed to a glossy tangerine shade that matched her outfit.

When Jon announced just before noon that he had everything he needed, Cooper had to admit she felt let down. As she slipped out of the wild orange pants and striped top they had her wear for the last batch of pictures, she realized it had been fun playing the part of a model. It was kind of sad to leave not knowing if she'd ever get a chance to do it again.

❋   ❋   ❋

This time when she arrived home, she patiently related every detail of the morning's events to her mother, who was taking an early lunch break. As she talked she helped herself to some of the Brie and crackers her mom had on a platter on the kitchen table. She had devoured a good amount of the cheese when Tara's comment about eating healthy came back to her again, and she pushed the high-fat snack out of her reach.

"What did they say when you were done? Did they give you any indication that they thought it went well?"

"I don't know," Cooper answered honestly, wracking her brain for some signal she might have missed from Jon or Brandi or the others. "*I* felt like it went well and it was actually pretty fun, but I don't have anything to compare it to."

"Well, I'm sure you did fine, honey," her mother assured her, giving her shoulder a pat. "I always thought you should be a model, even when you were a baby. You had such a pretty little face, not chubby like most babies, but beautiful."

"Thanks for the vote of confidence," Cooper said, caught a bit off guard by her mother's attempt at a compliment. "I guess we'll have to wait and see if Tara and her bosses agree with you."

"I just hope they don't keep us waiting too long," Mrs. Ellis replied.

❀   ❀   ❀

Cooper had just finished removing the morning's makeup when Alex arrived.

"Why don't you run down and pick up Claire?" she suggested, trying to buy a few minutes to reapply her makeup—but with a much lighter hand this time.

"I've already done that. She wasn't ready, either, so she sent me up here," he explained, a hint of exasperation in his voice.

"Well . . ." Cooper stalled. "Why don't you wait in the living room, then? Watch a little TV or something," she suggested helpfully. "I promise I'll be only a few minutes."

"Fine," he conceded with a loud sigh and a roll of his eyes.

"I'll hurry," Cooper vowed before gently pushing him back down the hall and into the Ellises' living room.

They had played out the same scene on countless Saturdays, and Cooper could never figure out why Alex was always so surprised when it happened again. He was always on time for things, and she and Claire were always late. The only reason Cooper made it to school on time was because of her mother's very necessary nagging. She did better with afternoon appointments or activities since they didn't usually involve getting out of bed. If she was already up, she could usually be wherever she needed to at the appointed hour. Because of this, she hoped that if she got the modeling contract that most of her appointments would be in the afternoon. If not, then she was going to have to learn to like—or at least tolerate—mornings.

"Okay, I'm ready," Cooper announced, making her way to where Alex sat engrossed in some cartoon. "No, really. I have my mittens on and everything," she said when Alex still hadn't budged.

When Claire arrived a few minutes after that, the girls had to physically drag Alex from the apartment.

"Wait! Just one more minute," he begged as they led him out to the elevator. "They were just getting to the good part!" Alex insisted, but the girls were deaf to his pleas.

On the way to Central Park, Cooper filled her friends in on her photo shoot, but she made them promise not to talk about it anymore after they arrived at the ice rink. She didn't want to be nervous all afternoon, wondering how the pictures were going to turn out.

Central Park was beautiful, and the three friends spent an enjoyable afternoon skating in circles and taking in the crisp New York air. The girls did, at least. Alex stayed pretty close to the wall, with the exception of the few occasions when he carefully ventured out to the center of the rink to join his friends.

"You're really doing much better," Claire told him as he stood perfectly still, balancing carefully on the thin silver blades.

"I'm ready for some hot chocolate or something," Alex announced, cautiously tottering over to Cooper. His sentence was barely spoken when his legs went out from under him. He quickly reached out and grabbed Cooper's sleeve on his way down, pulling her with him to the ice, where they both landed with an unceremonious *thud*.

"So am I *now*," Cooper replied. With Claire's help she managed to get up and brush off the cold, wet ice shavings that were clinging to her jeans. "I think you've definitely done enough damage here for one day," she told Alex, who was still flat on his back in the middle of the ice.

"I take absolutely no responsibility," he told her. "If you'll remember, this was not my idea."

"Yeah, whatever," Cooper responded before carefully helping him to his feet and off the ice to remove their skates.

Despite all his complaining, Cooper suspected Alex really did have a good time on their little skating outings. Even when he threatened to make the girls sit through a Jean-Claude Van Damme movie that night in retribution, she didn't take him seriously.

❊   ❊   ❊

At church on Sunday, Pastor Redding came through with several references for Alex to use in the reading group. Cooper and Claire had arrived with their parents, but as soon as church ended, they joined Alex on his quest. When the three approached their pastor after the late service, they had to wait almost fifteen minutes before he was free. Cooper had never realized how many people surrounded him after he preached, eager for a morsel of his time.

"It sounds like the group is going well," the pastor commented after Alex explained what he was after. "I think I can make several recommendations that will help you. If you want to stop by the office tomorrow, I could even loan you a few books."

"That would be great!" Alex told him. "I've never really done anything like this before, and I want to make sure I know what I'm talking about."

"That's the first step to being a great Bible study leader," Pastor Redding replied. "The fact that you're willing to admit when you don't know something already puts you a step ahead of a lot of people."

"I'll see you tomorrow, then," Alex said.

"Do you have the address?" Cooper questioned him as they walked away.

He flashed her his copy of that morning's bulletin with the church office's address printed on back. None of them had ever been to the office that, according to the bulletin, was about twenty blocks south of the college auditorium where the congregation met for its weekly services. Cooper wasn't surprised. Real estate prices in New York City were astronomical, and while it wasn't the most convenient arrangement, it was probably the best the medium-size church could do.

❋   ❋   ❋

Cooper was still thinking about what a nice weekend it had been when she dug out her homework that evening. Everything was perfect, almost like it used to be before Jana intruded. Cooper wished she didn't have to go back to school the next day and watch Jana continue to try to take away the people she cared about most. She wished it could just be the weekend forever. Rummaging through her backpack for her geometry book, Cooper's hand ran across an unfamiliar object. Pulling it out she realized it was Josh's CD. She had forgotten all about it after the disappointment of seeing him with Jana at the reading group.

Just one more thing Jana will probably take away, Cooper thought as she loaded the disc in her stereo and let the sweet-sounding music wash over her. *If he was ever really interested in the first place.*

THE TRANQUILLITY OF THE WEEKEND was broken at lunch on Monday when Cooper emerged from the cafeteria to find not only Jana and her friends, but also Josh camped out in her usual spot.

This situation just keeps getting worse and worse! a distraught Cooper thought.

And then, to make matters worse, as she was distributing the drinks to her friends, Jana said, "Oh, I'll have to give you my quarters tomorrow so you can get me a drink, too."

Cooper smiled as politely as she could and said "sure" through clenched teeth before sitting down to extricate her own lunch from its protective metal box. She tried hard to control her anger as she bit into her stuffed pita sandwich.

"So did you get a chance to listen to that *Eddie From Ohio* CD?" Josh asked right after Cooper had taken a huge bite. Mr. Robbins had surprised them with a pop quiz, so she hadn't been able to return the disc to Josh during biology, and now her mouth was too full to answer him. All she could do was nod her head.

Only after chewing for what seemed like hours and then taking a big gulp of her Diet Coke was she able to elaborate.

"I really liked it," Cooper told him. "Can you find them in record stores around here?"

"I think Tower down in SoHo should carry their stuff, but if not you can order it," he explained. "So you really liked it?" he asked again, seeming genuinely pleased.

"Enough to think about buying it," she told him. "Their lyrics are so poetic."

"Oooh! I want to see," Jana said, snatching the CD from Josh's hand and grabbing his attention, as well. "This looks cool," she told him after examining the cover art.

"You're welcome to borrow it if you want," Josh told her. "My brother turned me on to them."

"Thanks," Jana said, tucking the disc still warm from Cooper's bag into her own and giving Josh's arm an affectionate squeeze.

So much for thinking I meant anything special to him, Cooper told herself. *I think I'm safer keeping my crushes safely tucked away inside my head . . . like with Micah. I never have to actually have a conversation with him*, she decided.

Jana monopolized the rest of the lunchtime conversation with a story of some big concert she went to that past summer when she and her parents were vacationing in London. Of course, she had backstage passes and everything.

❋   ❋   ❋

More and more Cooper was finding herself relieved to arrive home after school. Each day seemed to bring some new change in the routine she had grown so used to and the friends she was so reluctant to share. She wasn't a selfish person, she just wanted things to stay the same forever—even though she knew in her heart they couldn't.

The ringing phone brought her back to the present, and she dropped her backpack, coat, and scarf in a heap on the entryway floor as she raced to answer it.

"Cooper Ellis, please," an unfamiliar voice requested.

"This is Cooper."

"Hi, Cooper, this is Tara at Yakomina. We got the proofs back from your test, and I'd like to go over them with you. Do you think you could come by the office?"

"I'm on my way," Cooper told her.

After scrawling a quick note for her parents, she stuffed her arms back into her coat and rushed out the door. The subway ride seemed to take forever as Cooper debated in her mind what Tara's comments had meant.

Maybe she didn't like the pictures and just wants to let me down easy, Cooper wondered. *But then again, she seems like a busy woman. She wouldn't take the time to see me if she didn't like them*, she reasoned. Her stomach was in knots by the time she reached the agency.

"Cooper Ellis to see Tara Jefferson," Cooper announced to the receptionist, hoping to sound a little more professional this time. It didn't seem to make any difference. The receptionist still waved Cooper to the waiting area without a word.

This time Tara came right out, though, and Cooper hadn't even heard the receptionist buzz her.

"I thought I heard your voice," Tara said. "Come on back. I bet you're anxious to see how your pictures turned out, huh?"

This time they didn't go to Tara's office but instead to a desk that could be illuminated at the end of the hall. Tara snapped on the light and set down a clear plastic sheet full of slides. When Cooper looked closer, she was barely able to make out more than a dozen little Coopers.

"Here, use this," Tara suggested, handing Cooper a small magnifier so that she could inspect the pictures. She quickly leaned over the desk and put her eye up to the glass to get a better look.

"Wow!" Cooper exclaimed after looking at several of the pictures. "I barely even recognize myself."

"Is that a good thing or a bad thing?" Tara teased.

"I'm not sure," Cooper answered honestly.

"You may be undecided, but I'm really happy with how the shoot went. For someone with no experience, you come across very well, and if you're interested we'd like to sign you."

"Really?" Cooper asked, not sure she had heard Tara right.

"Yes, we'd like to sign you to a modeling contract," Tara repeated. "Why don't we go to my office and I can explain what that means. Also, I have some information for you to take home to your parents."

"Oh, of course," Cooper replied, still a little stunned.

When she left the office half an hour later, clutching an envelope full of information for her parents to read over and a copy of her pictures, she was still in a fog. Even when she got home and showed her mother the "contact sheet," as Tara had called her photos, it still seemed a little unreal.

"This calls for a celebration!" her mother declared. "Let me call your father and see if he wants to meet us somewhere."

Cooper just smiled before scrutinizing the pictures again.

"Daddy's going to meet us at Tatou in an hour. How does that sound?" her mother asked, more as a formality than really for the sake of getting Cooper's input. Not that Cooper had a better suggestion in mind. Tatou was pricey and elegant and just the kind of place for a celebration.

"I'll call and make the reservation, but first do you want to call Claire and invite her along? I'm sure she'll be so excited for you," her mother continued when Cooper failed to respond to her first question.

"I guess so," Cooper agreed, taking the cordless phone from her mother and dialing Claire's number.

"Claire, guess what?" Cooper said as soon as her friend picked up. "I got offered the modeling contract! Can you believe it?"

"Oh, Cooper, that's great!"

"Mom and I are meeting Dad at Tatou for dinner to celebrate and you're invited."

"When are you going?" Claire asked, suddenly sounding a little strange.

"We're meeting him in an hour, so I guess we'll leave in about forty-five minutes," Cooper told her.

"I'm really sorry, but I can't," Claire responded.

"What do you mean?" a bewildered Cooper asked. "I don't want to celebrate without my best friend. You know your parents will let you go if my mom talks to them."

"It's not that . . . it's just that Jana is coming by for a fitting, and if I don't do it tonight, I won't have her dress finished in time for the wedding she's going to this weekend."

"Couldn't you call her and ask her to come later?" Cooper pleaded.

"I would, but she wasn't going to be home. She's coming by here on her way home from dance class. I can't just not be here."

"Don't worry about it," Cooper said resignedly. Suddenly, she didn't feel much like celebrating anymore, either.

"If I had a little notice, I could have changed my plans. I'm really sorry, Cooper."

And Cooper knew she honestly was, but that did little to cheer her up. "I guess I'll see you in the morning, then."

"I guess you will," Claire said. "And again, congratulations, Cooper. I'm really proud of you."

"Thanks," Cooper mumbled right before she turned the phone off.

"So is it dinner for four?" her mom asked.

"No, just three," Cooper told her. "Claire has other plans."

"Oh, honey, I'm sorry. Maybe you'd like to call and invite Alex?"

"No, that's all right. It's no big deal."

"Whatever you want, dear. Now, why don't you run and change? Your short gray velvet dress would be nice. It brings out your eyes."

Cooper wandered off to her room, not really caring what she wore to dinner. The excitement of the evening had been ruined . . . by Jana. Just like so many other things lately.

I know it's not her fault, Cooper thought as she slipped the dress her mother had suggested over her head. *She had no idea I was going to invite Claire to dinner tonight. But still, she seems to have a habit of popping up at the most inopportune moments. And I never even saw her talk to Josh until the day I started to think I might be interested. It's like one horrible coincidence after another.*

Cooper tried to block it out of her mind as she put on a pair of shimmery gray tights and buckled her black-patent Mary Janes with the chunky heels. Her favorite antique silver necklace finished off the look. Then with a little blush, some berry-colored lip stain, and a quick comb of her hair she was ready. At least she looked festive even if she didn't feel it.

"Don't you look nice," Mrs. Ellis said when Cooper returned to the living room. "I just need to grab my purse and I'm ready to go. Why don't you bring the pictures to show your dad?" she suggested.

Cooper stuffed the photos back in the manila envelope and carried it with her out the door, down the elevator, and into the taxi they hailed in front of their building.

Her father was already there when they arrived. "So I hear you have big news, eh, shorty?" he teased. He'd been calling her shorty ever since she sprouted up to five six in the fifth grade. He wasn't exactly on the short side, either, but that didn't stop him from teasing her. Cooper knew it was only his way of being affectionate. For some reason, her dad could say things that coming from her mom would cause her to bristle.

"You have to see these pictures, Jack. She looks breathtaking," Mrs. Ellis gushed. "I can't believe our little baby could look so grown-up."

"If you're going to get all mushy, I'm moving to another table," Cooper threatened.

"I'll try to contain myself," her mother promised. "Now, why don't you show Daddy your pictures."

Cooper pulled the contact sheets out of their protective envelope and passed them to her father.

"Looks like you found another use for that height besides playing basketball" was the first thing her father said.

"Very funny," Cooper told him, rolling her eyes. For years she had been fighting off coaches who were sure that if Cooper just gave it a chance she'd really love the sport. One gym teacher even had the nerve to tell her it was a crime to waste the "genetic gift" she'd been given by not playing. Her father had gotten a real kick out of that one. The truth was, though,

Cooper was the most unathletic person she knew. It wouldn't matter if she were tall enough to tower over the basket, she'd find some other way to mess up the game. Sports were definitely not her thing.

"Seriously, Cooper, you look very beautiful in these pictures," her dad leaned close and whispered just as their waiter arrived with their drinks. "But I think you look beautiful without your hair and makeup all done, too," he added.

Cooper flashed her dad one of her warmest smiles. *Sometimes he knows the exact thing to say*, she thought.

"Hey, I thought Claire was going to join us. What happened?" he suddenly asked.

Then again, sometimes he doesn't. "She had to do a fitting for this dress she's making for a girl at school," Cooper explained, trying hard not to sound bothered by her best friend's absence.

"That's too bad. I'm sure she wanted to be here."

"No, it's fine, really," Cooper insisted.

Her mother was only halfway through telling her father all the details of Cooper's new job when their food came. As her mother continued to talk, Cooper poked at her chicken and moved her potatoes around on her plate. She was busy segregating her mixed vegetables when she heard her dad addressing her.

"Cooper, are you sure modeling is something you really want to do? You don't seem very happy about it."

"Huh? I'm sorry, what did you say?" Cooper asked, trying to snap herself out of her reverie. He hadn't even finished repeating the question when Cooper began protesting.

"No, that's not it. I'm excited about the modeling thing— at least I think I am. It just feels kind of weird to be out celebrating the fact that I photograph well," she admitted. "I mean, it's not like I worked really hard and got a good grade or something. I'm being rewarded for being tall and having good bone structure."

"To a degree you're right, but I don't think you'd last long in this job or any other if that's all you have going for you," her dad pointed out. "I think that modeling agency saw what a responsible young woman you are, and they were impressed with those pictures because in addition to your outer beauty, they saw your inner beauty shining through. Not every beautiful woman has that going for her."

"That's funny . . . because I haven't felt very beautiful on the inside lately," Cooper admitted.

"What are you talking about?" her mother asked, a note of distress in her voice.

Only then did Cooper relate to them the problems she'd been having at school lately and how upset she was at Jana for turning her life upside down. "Every day she seems to find some new way to annoy me."

"That doesn't sound like you," her father said. "Have you ever thought that maybe Jana really needs you to be her friend?"

"Ha! That is soooo not the case! She has a million friends. People flock around her all the time at school. I'm the one who's going to need friends when this is all over."

"Just because she's always surrounded by people doesn't mean she has friends. It can be very lonely being popular and having people like you for *what* you are rather than *who* you are. You're very fortunate to have Claire and Alex, even if Claire couldn't drop everything to be here tonight. Most people don't have such loyal friends. I can see why Jana would be so drawn to them."

"I just don't know why she had to pick us," Cooper complained.

"It could be you're looking at this backward. Maybe she didn't do the picking," Mr. Ellis said. "Maybe Someone picked you for Jana because He knew how much you had to give."

"Is that your subtle way of suggesting that *God* wants me to be nice to Jana? You're starting to sound like Alex with his theories about how we can change the whole school with our little reading group."

"Well, maybe you can. Stranger things have happened," her dad suggested. "You could at least give it a try."

"I'll think about it," Cooper agreed.

"Now that we've got that settled, who's up for some tiramisu?" Mrs. Ellis asked. "A celebration isn't a celebration without dessert!"

IN BED THAT NIGHT Cooper recalled a sermon Pastor Redding had preached a few weeks earlier. The topic was loving your enemies, something she'd heard about at least a dozen times over the years. It hadn't seemed particularly pertinent before, but in light of her conversation with her father over dinner, she thought she should take another look. Not that she really thought of Jana as an enemy, but she knew her attitude toward Jana could use some work.

Snapping her bedside light back on, Cooper grabbed her Bible from her night table and began flipping through the pages, looking for old bulletins. She came across four of them and a large assortment of bookmarks and other scraps of paper before finding what she was looking for. It was folded in half and tucked in between Luke chapters six and seven, her notes scrawled in its margin, curving around that morning's worship choruses and announcements.

"Anyone who claims to be in the light but hates his brother is still in the darkness," 1 John 2:9 said. She had also copied down Matthew 5:44–45: "Love your enemies and pray for those that persecute you, that you may be sons of your father in heaven."

Funny how they weren't the least bit convicting a few

weeks ago, but now Cooper felt a knot forming in the pit of her stomach. Maybe her dad was right. Maybe Jana really did need some good friends, and Cooper certainly wasn't making things easy on her. Scanning her notes she found something else Pastor Redding had said that she hadn't paid much attention to at the time.

"If you only love the people who love you, you've done nothing special. How hard is that?" he'd asked and Cooper had copied down. *"But loving those who are hard for you to love, that's a sign of spiritual maturity."*

There was more, but it had been obliterated by a series of hearts and triangles Cooper had drawn around the pastor's words. Sometimes it was hard to pay attention throughout the whole service after sitting in classes all week listening to her teachers, no matter how much she wanted to. She had to admit she sometimes found herself doodling between Pastor Redding's points, but she sure wished she could go back now and pay closer attention to that particular sermon.

"God, please help me to be nice to Jana no matter how horribly she treats me," Cooper whispered from her perch on the end of her bed. "And give me an extra helping of self-control this week, if you could, so I don't react so quickly when she does something to provoke me. Most of all, let her see your love in me."

After turning out the light and crawling back under the covers, Cooper added one final thing. "And, God, I'm sorry for not praying about this sooner. I really do want to do the right thing."

❋　　❋　　❋

Bracing herself all morning for the persecution she was

sure she would endure when she tried to reach out to Jana, Cooper kept silently repeating Luke 6:22 in her mind. *Blessed are you when men hate you, blessed are you when men hate you, blessed are you when men hate you, blessed are you when* . . . The words took on a comforting rhythm and made her feel a little better about what was to come, and she clung to them until she arrived at the Coke machine after biology class.

There she repeated another verse to herself. It was the most practical one she had found the night before while running over her sermon notes: Romans 12:20. "If your enemy is hungry, feed him." Reading it had immediately brought to mind Jana's words from the previous day about having Cooper get her a drink, too. While it was a small thing, really, buying Jana a drink seemed like the perfect gesture to show her attitude had changed. So after wasting several precious minutes of her lunch period in the drink line, Cooper made her way out to the courtyard carefully balancing four drinks and her lunch box.

"All right! Toss the root beer here," Alex yelled as soon as Cooper came into view.

Jana, Blake, Anne, Lindsay, and Josh were there, too, their presence becoming the rule rather than exception it seemed. But Cooper was ready. She sat down next to Claire, handing her friend her usual drink, then turned to Jana and held a can out to her.

"I hope diet's okay," Cooper said.

"I usually get caffeine-free, but I guess this will do," Jana said. She took the can and popped it open, then went back to ignoring Cooper like she usually did. Obviously, she found Josh much more interesting and was engrossed in writing her name on his hand with a silver felt pen. She didn't even offer to pay for the drink.

"That was really nice of you," Claire whispered to Cooper once they had finally begun eating.

"It's the new and improved me," Cooper replied.

"Well, you certainly tried," Alex admitted, "but you're right, she does give you the cold shoulder." He said it low enough that Jana and the others couldn't hear. Cooper only shrugged her shoulders.

"It doesn't really matter. I'm not responsible for how other people treat me, only how I treat them." She went on to explain, sharing a bit of enlightenment with her friends.

"This really *is* a new and improved you," Claire said, obviously impressed.

"And I hear there have been some other changes, too," Alex said. "Why didn't you call me last night?"

"What? Oh, you mean the modeling contract. I can't believe I completely forgot about it until right now!"

"Are you serious? How do you forget something like that?" Alex asked.

"I've had a lot on my mind this morning, I guess," Cooper explained. "And I would have called, but everything happened so fast. I didn't think you'd really be into dinner out with my parents anyway."

"That's fine," he told her. "But now I want to hear everything. When will you be on the cover of *Vogue* or *Elle*?" She had already given Claire the details on the way to school, but Alex hadn't been filled in.

"I wouldn't count on seeing me on any covers any time soon. Right now Tara just wants me to try to get as many pictures in my book as possible. That means I get sent out on a lot of "go-sees" with tons of other girls and hope the editors or whoever hires the models like how I look."

"Even Elle MacPherson had to start somewhere," Alex pointed out.

"But I am *not* Elle MacPherson," Cooper protested. "Although I think that's obvious without me pointing it out."

"Yeah, but I hear they can really do a lot with makeup these days," Alex teased.

"Thanks for the encouragement!"

"Any time. That's what friends are for."

"What was that about Elle MacPherson?" Jana asked, suddenly tuning in to the conversation.

"Alex was comparing Cooper to her," Claire explained.

"Why?" Jana practically scoffed.

"That's exactly what I said," Cooper agreed good-naturedly, pretending not to notice Jana's rudeness. The response seemed to stun her into a momentary silence. Before Jana could speak again, Claire tried to further explain.

"Cooper was offered a modeling contract, so Alex was joking about her becoming a supermodel."

"Really?" Jana asked. "You were offered a modeling contract? Which agency?"

It was one of the only times Jana had addressed her directly, and Cooper was determined to make the most of it. "It's just a small agency called Yakomina Models," she explained. "And I haven't even signed the contract yet. I needed to have my parents look at it first."

"That's kind of cool," Jana said, her face changing instantaneously from the usual look of disinterest it wore when the subject was Cooper. "I took some modeling classes a couple of years ago, but I never really pursued it," she added coolly.

"My mom tried to get me to do that when I was in junior high," Cooper admitted. "I just felt too awkward, though. In fact, I still do sort of. I'm not at all sure anyone will actually hire me for anything, but the agency convinced me to give it a try."

"They must think you can get work or they wouldn't be wasting their time," Jana replied in a matter-of-fact way. "I'm sure you'll be great."

Cooper was stunned by how supportive Jana was suddenly being. She had hoped that by making an effort to be friendly she might eventually win Jana over or that at some point Jana might start to at least be civil to her, but this had been too easy!

"I guess we'll see soon," Cooper told her.

❈　　❈　　❈

Things just got better and better between Cooper and Jana. The next day at lunch, to Cooper's amazement, Jana met her at the Coke machine and kept her company in line, then walked out to the courtyard with her.

That afternoon she walked home with Cooper and Claire since she needed to have a final fitting for her new dress, and she couldn't seem to get enough information about Cooper. Her favorite movie, TV show, food, way to spend a Saturday. It was almost exhausting, but Cooper answered each question with a feeling of satisfaction. She had done the right thing reaching out to Jana, and now God was rewarding her. It was a great feeling.

"Why don't you come with us to Claire's?" Jana suggested. "I'd love for you to see the dress. It looked great the last time I saw it."

"I promised Tara at the modeling agency I'd check in with her first thing after school," Cooper explained. "She wants to get me going out on calls as soon as possible."

"So run upstairs and call her, then come back down," Jana persisted.

"I can't. After I call her it's time for my monthly room-cleaning session. When it gets to the point where every square inch of carpet is covered, my mom insists I clean it."

"Well, maybe I'll stop by after the fitting, then," Jana told her. "You'll probably need a little break."

"Sure, if you want to," Cooper shrugged.

"I'll see you in a bit," Jana promised as she and Claire got out of the elevator.

❄   ❄   ❄

Tara didn't have any news about jobs for Cooper, but Cooper hadn't really expected her to. It was just good for Cooper to get in the habit of checking in. Beepers weren't allowed in Cooper's high school, so once she started getting work, assuming she did start getting work, she would need to begin checking in with Tara each afternoon before leaving school to see if she had any appointments she needed to race off to. Still, it was fun to hear about the progress of her pictures—Tara said they would have them back and in her portfolio by the end of the week—and she had heard back from the editor of the salon magazine, who was very pleased with Cooper's photo session, so those pictures would go in her book, as well.

When Jana rang the doorbell an hour later, Cooper was halfway through cleaning her room, and as Jana had predicted, she was more than ready for a break.

"Come in and save me from the bottomless pit!" she cried as she opened the door and invited Jana inside. "No matter how much I pick up, there always seems to be more!"

"It's a good thing I showed up when I did, then, isn't it?"

"Definitely. I deserve a break," Cooper insisted, trying hard to make Jana feel more welcome than the last time she had come over. "Do you want something to drink? How about something to eat? My mother always buys tons of food even though there are only three of us."

"Anything would be fine. I am a little hungry."

"Well, there's ice cream," Cooper suggested, pulling out two containers of Haagen Dazs. "Or how about some Mint Milano cookies?"

"What are you having?" Jana asked, undecided.

"I think I'll opt for some raspberry sorbet," Cooper told her.

"Then that's what I'll have, too," Jana chimed in agreeably.

"Are you sure?" Cooper questioned.

"No, sorbet is fine. If you show me where your ice cream scoop is, I'll even help dish it up."

As they sat in the living room watching an ancient episode of *Speed Racer* on the television, Cooper couldn't believe how much had changed in her life in the last twenty-four hours. She had a new job, a new friend, and a newfound spiritual maturity. *And to think I used to hate change*, she thought. *I sure am glad I'm over that once and for all!*

COOPER'S WEEK CONTINUED to improve. With her newly
clean room, she was able to easily find everything she
needed for school on Thursday morning without rushing
around like usual. It was almost enough to cause her to re-
pent of her messy ways for good. Almost.

In biology that day, Josh was especially nice to her, and
at lunch when Alex brought up the idea of going out to a
movie on Friday night—the new Sundance Film Festival win-
ner was opening—Cooper thought the change from their
routine was a great idea and personally invited Jana, Josh,
and everyone to come along. Claire and Alex just smiled at
their "changed" friend.

In the reading group that afternoon, letter nine dealt with
another heavy topic: Why God doesn't always physically in-
tervene when bad things happen.

"Why didn't He stop the *Titanic* from hitting that iceberg
in order to save all those helpless people from dying?" Alex
asked. "Why didn't He stop Hitler from massacring so many
Jews during World War II?"

Cooper's life was going so well, everything was so close
to perfect, that she found she almost had trouble relating to
the topic. But remembering the sermon on loving your

enemies, she made a special effort to pay attention and file the information away for future reference. She knew that it could very well come in handy at some later date.

"In the book, C. S. Lewis, through Screwtape, explains how God takes away His hand to teach His children to walk," Alex continued. "He's like a parent who lets His toddler risk falling down in order to eventually take a few steps."

"But if I fell into a pool when I was learning to walk, my parents would have jumped in to save me," Jana pointed out. "Why doesn't God do that?"

"Maybe He does in some ways," Claire replied. She didn't always speak up, but when she did, her comments were usually well thought out and pretty deep. "You may not feel Him physically pull you out of the water, but I bet He's rescued you more times than you know. Still, you have to remember, it isn't always His will that we be rescued. Sometimes He is willing to let us go through really hard things because those experiences are what make us grow. But when that happens we whine and complain only because we can't see the ultimate result like He can."

"So why doesn't He just show us the ultimate result so we'll understand?" Jana wondered aloud.

"Because He wants us to trust Him without having to know everything. He wants us to obey even when we don't understand," Cooper said, taking her turn fielding one of their new friend's many questions.

"But that's too hard. I don't think I can do that," Jana admitted. "More important, I don't know if I *want* to do that."

"That's a decision you have to make for yourself," Alex said. It was clear by the look on Jana's face that that wasn't the answer she wanted to hear. "That's the whole point of having a free will. God gives you the choice. Just like Hitler had a choice and the captain of the *Titanic* had a choice. God doesn't want us to be puppets, so He lets us decide to follow Him or not. And Screwtape and Wormwood are always there trying to make us doubt."

The complex discussion had made the afternoon pass quickly, and Cooper couldn't believe it when Alex said their time was up. All the way home she couldn't stop thinking about Jana and how full of questions she always was. Before, she had found the questions annoying and antagonistic. Now Cooper saw something deeper. Jana really seemed to be searching for something to believe in.

Earlier in the week Cooper had been so convinced that God wanted her to reach out to Jana and be her friend, but what if He wanted more? Hadn't her dad said just the other night that he thought God had brought her into Jana's life for a reason? Maybe that reason was bigger than she thought at first. Maybe she was supposed to help Jana learn to trust God!

Filled with a new sense of purpose, Cooper strolled down Columbus Avenue feeling lighter than air. She couldn't wait to see what was going to happen next. She couldn't wait to see Jana again and begin her mission.

There was a message from Tara on the machine when she got home that said she needed Cooper to call the agency immediately. Hoping nothing was wrong, Cooper pulled Tara's wrinkled business card out of her backpack where she kept it now and dialed.

"Tara, this is Cooper. What's up?" she said when her booker was finally on the line.

"I have two appointments lined up for you tomorrow!" Tara told her, excitement tinging her voice. "You have to stop by here on your way, though, to pick up your portfolio so you have it for your appointments. I've got the pictures from the test and the salon in it already, and it looks good."

"That's great!" Cooper replied. "I'll be over right after school," she promised.

"Good, I'll give you the rest of the information then," Tara said, then before hanging up added, "Girl, it looks like you are on your way!"

"Well, thanks" was all Cooper could think of to say to that. "I'll see you tomorrow."

After hanging up the phone, she called her mother at the interior design shop to tell her the news.

"Honey, that's fantastic. What are you going to wear?"

"I just got off the phone with Tara, Mom. I haven't had time to really think about it yet."

"Well, I think your black jumper would look nice with your new tights and your black shoes," Mrs. Ellis suggested. "You can't ever go wrong with black."

"Except at a wedding," Cooper joked.

"Just promise me you won't wear those hideous black boots," her mother pleaded. "They make you look like you're a new recruit in the army."

"I promise," Cooper agreed. "Anyway, we can talk about it when you get home. Do you want me to start something for dinner?"

"No, that's all right. I was downtown today, so I picked up some pasta salad with chicken from Dean & Deluca. I also got some really nice asparagus and a loaf of ciabatta bread. I'll be home soon with it, so don't spoil your appetite."

"Okay. I'll see you when you get here," Cooper told her.

❊   ❊   ❊

For the second consecutive Friday, Cooper rushed out the

front doors of Hudson High and down the steps, off to another world. She took a cab again, afraid the subway would make her late for her first appointment. Too many times when she had somewhere in particular to be, her subway train would be unexpectedly delayed, and she wasn't taking any chances today.

Entering the Yakomina offices, Cooper felt completely at ease. She belonged there now. It seemed like even the receptionist knew because she didn't motion for Cooper to have a seat but sent her back to Tara's office immediately. She even spoke without using hand signals, looking up from her work as she did so. And Cooper's book was just as wonderful as Tara had said. The pictures really had come out beautifully.

"I know this sounds so dumb, but I'm surprised by how professional they look," Cooper confessed.

"That's what we're going for," Tara told her with a laugh. "You'll learn after a while to be able to look at a sheet of proofs and pick out the ones that convey that, too. It just takes time and experience. And speaking of experience, if you're going to get any, you'd better get going," she said.

With her portfolio stowed safely in her bag and the addresses of the two offices she was to visit tucked in her pocket, Cooper made her way back out onto the crowded Manhattan streets. The first stop was close enough she could walk. Just eight blocks up and one over.

According to Tara's note, she was going to a magazine's editorial offices. When the elevator dumped her out in the middle of their reception area, Cooper knew that meant the publication took up the entire floor of the high-rise building she was in. She tried not to feel intimidated by her surroundings and had to remind herself not to stare at the huge glossy copies of the covers that were mounted on the walls or at all the important-looking people busily streaming past her.

After just a few minutes of waiting, she was led around a maze of corners, past a large board that had color copies of magazine pages covered with handwritten notes and revisions taped to it. Finally, they reached an office that looked a lot like Tara's. Pictures of models lined the walls, and what space wasn't covered by them was filled in with stories or headlines clipped from magazines, as well as some greeting cards and personal notes.

"Hi, I'm April," a woman with thick auburn hair said, holding out a hand to Cooper.

"Cooper . . . Ellis," Cooper replied as she tried to seem calm and convey an air of confidence she didn't necessarily feel.

"Why don't you come on in and have a seat?" April suggested. "This is my assistant, Fiona."

Cooper took a seat in a black leather chair next to April's messy desk and pulled her new portfolio out of the black tote bag her mother had come home with the night before. It was a modeling present, she had said. She had read in a magazine that this was the new bag all the models couldn't live without this season and insisted that Cooper would need something a little more professional than her backpack as she went out on appointments.

"Tara says you're just starting out," April commented, paging through the few shots in Cooper's book. "How did you get into this crazy business?"

Cooper related the highlights of her story to the women, adding a few details like how nervous she had been when Medea suggested she cut off most of her hair. She even told them about the toenail polish mishap. After she had shared those stories, she wondered if maybe they weren't the kinds of things she should have told them—if maybe they made her seem less professional, but Fiona quickly put her at ease.

"Yes, it's a whole different world," Fiona agreed, then laughingly added, "a world where your toenails are not your own."

Cooper smiled gratefully. They asked a few more questions—where Cooper went to school, her favorite subject, how long she had lived in New York—before getting to the point.

"Okay, now, can you stand up for us?" April asked.

Once Cooper had complied, they gave her several directions. She felt a little like a show pony, but she did as they asked. First, she was instructed to pull her hair off her face, then turn to the left and the right, and finally, to walk across the room several times and smile for them.

Soon there was another girl with the same coloring as Cooper standing in the doorway. She was obviously April and Fiona's next appointment so they said good-bye, and Cooper was left to find her own way out of the maze of hallways and back to the elevator. She was still wandering down the corridors when she heard her name being called.

"Cooper, wait! We forgot to get a card from you," Fiona was saying.

Cooper, not knowing what she meant, pulled Tara's battered business card from her bag and handed it over.

"Here you go," she said. "Sorry it's a little beat up, but it's the only one I have. I guess I'll have to get more the next time I'm in the office."

Fiona began to laugh, but Cooper couldn't figure out why. Finally the assistant explained that a "card" was something each model had printed up with her name, vital statistics, agency contact, and a least one head shot and full-length picture of herself. That way editors could remember who they had seen.

"You really are new at this, aren't you?" Fiona asked, still unable to completely stop laughing.

"This was my first appointment," Cooper admitted, feeling extremely young and inexperienced.

"It will get easier. I'm sure your agency is getting cards printed up for you, so don't worry about it. Besides, I don't think I'll have trouble remembering you without a photo this one time."

Cooper was sure that was not a good thing. She could just imagine Fiona going back into April's office and telling her about the crumpled business card Cooper had handed her. They would never hire someone so inexperienced.

How long will it be before I know enough to not make a fool of myself at appointments? she wondered as she headed off to meet with the next editors. She was already cringing as she imagined all the horrible things she could possibly do there. She hadn't thought modeling would be such a mine-field. *And someone as clumsy as me is destined to just keep stepping on them*, Cooper thought unhappily.

"HEY, COOPER!" JANA called out from the line in front of the theater. "Over here!"

"We thought you weren't going to make it," Alex told her when she finally joined them.

"Sorry, I had no idea how long those appointments were going to take . . . and then there was a problem on the subway, and I had to go all the way downtown and change trains just to get back up here."

"Well, you're here now and that's what's important," Claire insisted.

"So tell us all about your appointments," Jana asked. "Where were they? Did you get the jobs?"

Cooper politely answered Jana's questions, telling her about the misunderstanding with the card at the magazine and how the second place spent thirty minutes talking to her before telling her unceremoniously that she wasn't "intriguing enough" for what they were shooting.

"They actually said that to your face?" an incredulous Claire asked. "How rude!"

"That's what I thought," Cooper agreed, but she was able to laugh about it now.

"You should have taken those modeling classes," Jana

told her. "We learned all about cards and books and everything."

"I know. I'm probably the only girl in all of New York City who didn't know what they meant when they asked for my card."

"No, you're not. I wouldn't have had any idea what they were talking about, either," Claire chimed in, trying to comfort her friend.

Cooper didn't really care. She figured she'd eventually get the hang of it, and if she didn't, she was no worse off than before. After all, there were definitely more important things in life than modeling. Like friends, for one. And Cooper was surrounded by those as she entered the dimly lit movie theater, happily chomping on her unbuttered popcorn.

"Can I see your book?" Jana asked once they were seated. There was little room to maneuver in the tight rows, but Cooper managed to reach down and pull the black leather-covered album from her new bag. On the front, "Yakomina Models" was embossed in a silver, important-looking script.

"Wow, these don't even look like you," Jana announced loudly, squinting at the pictures in the bad theater light.

"I know, that's what everyone who sees them says. I still can't figure out if that's good or bad."

"No, they're great," Jana insisted. "What photographers did you work with? Were they big names?"

"I have no idea," Cooper said with a shrug. "I mean, I know their first names, Jean-Paul and Jon, but I don't know what else they've done."

"You don't mean Jon Marron, do you?" Jana excitedly quizzed her friend.

"Maybe, I mean that sounds sort of right. I know his last name started with an *M*."

"Cooper! He's a big deal!" Jana practically shouted. "I can't believe you didn't know this!"

"I guess it's just one of the many things I have to learn."

"I think you should hire me as your coach," Jana suggested, handing the portfolio back to Cooper just as the lights went down.

Cooper couldn't tell if Jana was serious or not, so she said nothing and instead concentrated on tucking the book carefully back inside her bag.

❉   ❉   ❉

The phone rang much too early the next morning. Cooper had really been looking forward to sleeping in after missing out the previous weekend, and if it had been up to her she would have just let it ring, but her mother always picked up.

"Cooper, it's Jana," her mother announced from the doorway.

"Mmm-hmn—huh," she moaned from under layers of blankets.

"Cooper!" her mother repeated a little more loudly. "You have a call."

Knowing she wasn't going to have any peace until she took the receiver, she reached one arm out from under the mound of bedding and waved it around. Her mom gave her the cordless phone, and Cooper pulled it back inside her little cocoon.

"This better be extremely important," Cooper mumbled once she had the phone up to her ear.

"Oh, did I wake you up?" Jana asked innocently.

"What time is it?"

"Ten. Why?" Jana asked.

"I don't want to open my eyes and look at my own clock because I don't want to wake up any more than necessary," Cooper explained. "I'm going right back to sleep when we're done."

"But I was going to come over! Come on. You've had enough sleep for one night," Jana pleaded. "I have something to show you, and then I thought maybe we could go down to The Cupping Room and look for the love of my life."

"The Cupping Room is open at night, too, isn't it?" Cooper hinted, but then she remembered her new mission and wondered if maybe God wasn't giving her an opportunity to spend time with Jana so they could talk! Before Jana could persuade any further, Cooper did an about-face and said, "I'm getting up as we speak."

"Great, I'll be over in an hour," Jana replied, not even questioning Cooper's sudden change of attitude.

Cooper was so happy with how well her week had gone that once she was up and moving she didn't even mind not sleeping in that much. Then, to her mother's great delight, she ate several slices of melon before she headed to the shower, humming a song she couldn't place. It wasn't until she was shaving her legs that she remembered it was a tune from the CD Josh had loaned her. He had been sitting on the other side of Jana at the movies the night before, and Cooper couldn't help but notice that they didn't really seem interested in each other. *Maybe I should just come out and ask Jana if she likes him*, Cooper thought as she dried off.

Her hair was still wet, but she had her makeup on and was dressed when Jana arrived. Her room was still relatively clean and she even had her portfolio, the health and beauty book Tara had given her, and Tara's business card stacked neatly on her desk since all she needed was to have something happen to her portfolio. She wasn't sure, but she doubted it was something she could get replaced, and she knew that if there was any way to spill something on it she would.

"So you're not a morning person, huh?" Jana asked, peering her head into Cooper's bedroom. Mrs. Ellis had let her into the apartment on her way to work at the design shop.

"Not in the least," Cooper unapologetically replied.

"Then I'm honored you got up for me."

"I had something I wanted to talk to you about," Cooper told her, whispering a quick prayer so she would say the right thing.

"Really? What?"

"Well, you seemed to have a lot of questions the other day in the reading group and I thought maybe I could answer some of them," Cooper offered.

"I did? I don't really remember," Jana said, suddenly looking uncomfortable.

"Yeah, you weren't sure you really wanted to trust God or that you could trust God," Cooper reminded, refusing to let the subject go.

"Oh, I guess I did say that."

"At least take a look at this book," Cooper encouraged her, handing her a copy of Josh McDowell's *More Than a Carpenter*, which Cooper had read the previous year. "It might explain things better than I can."

"Fine," Jana agreed, seeming anxious to put an end to the uncomfortable discussion. "And now I have something to talk to you about," she announced.

"Oh! Well, that's great," Cooper enthused, sure that now Jana was going to bare her soul.

"Actually, it's really something I wanted to show you," she corrected.

Jana's words seemed to jog her memory. "You mentioned something about that on the phone, didn't you?"

"Uh-huh," Jana said, smoothing Cooper's unmade bed before sprawling across it. "These are from that modeling class," she went on to explain as she spread out several books and folders on the bed. "Remember I told you last night that I had some things that might be helpful?"

Cooper joined Jana on the bed and began rummaging through the stuff. The thick folder she picked up next had the name of the school on the front, and inside it had, among other things, a glossary of modeling terms. *That might be helpful*, Cooper thought, but much of the rest of the information seemed like common sense.

"I thought you might want to make a copy of that," Jana said, peering over Cooper's shoulder.

"Thanks. That would be great," Cooper answered, setting the pages on her desk.

"Now do you want to see the pictures I had done?"

"Sure," Cooper said, taking the book Jana offered.

As Cooper paged through the shots, comments Tara had made when they were looking at her own pictures kept coming to mind. The pictures were nice and Jana looked very pretty, but Cooper knew Tara would say they looked too much like portraits rather than actual editorial shots. There had been several pictures in Cooper's proofs that she thought looked better than the ones Tara chose, but her agent patiently explained what it was about each that made them not quite right. At the time, Cooper hadn't thought she'd understood very well, but now it was clear she had taken in more than she'd realized.

"So . . . what do you think?" Jana asked expectantly.

"They're really nice," Cooper replied, trying to sound enthusiastic. "You look great in them." Even as she spoke, though, she was trying frantically to find some way to steer the conversation back around to spiritual things. *God, you wanted me to do this, so why are you making it so difficult?* she prayed.

"I'm glad you think so because I wanted to ask you something."

"Shoot," Cooper said, looking expectantly at the pretty blonde. Maybe now she could get things back on track.

"I was thinking of trying to get into modeling, too, and I thought you might put in a good word for me," Jana blurted out.

"Oh," Cooper said, her brow furrowing in concern. That wasn't what she had expected to hear at all.

"So will you?" Jana prodded.

"I don't know what you think I can do," Cooper told her honestly. "I haven't been hired for anything myself yet. It's not as if I have any clout in the business."

"But you do have an agent *and* a contract," Jana pointed out. "I'm sure if you told them you thought I'd be great, they'd sign me, too. Or at least they'd agree to meet with me."

Cooper was the first to admit she was no expert on modeling, but Jana couldn't be more than five five. And while she was certainly pretty, she had a round face rather than the angular look that seemed popular with designers.

"Are you sure you're right for modeling?" Cooper asked, hoping she might tactfully dissuade Jana.

"What do you mean? Don't you think I have what it takes?" Jana challenged.

"It's not that," Cooper backpedaled, anxious to not

offend her friend. "I just wonder if you're tall enough." She had picked the least critical comment she could find and sighed in relief at having averted a disaster.

"They used to say that before Kate Moss became a supermodel, too, and she's only three inches taller than I am."

"Three inches is quite a bit, though," Cooper gently pointed out.

"I'm just asking you to put in a good word for me," Jana repeated. "You act like I asked you to give me your right arm or something."

"No, that's not it. I just don't want you to get your hopes up. It's really competitive, and they turn away lots of beautiful girls every day for little things like a few inches," Cooper explained, repeating part of the speech Tara had given her during her first meeting.

"I think you just don't want me to model because I might be better at it than you," Jana spat back.

"That's not it at all!" Cooper almost shouted, hoping the sheer volume with which she said the words would convince Jana. This whole morning was not going anything like Cooper had planned. *God, where are you?* she frantically asked as she glanced at the ceiling.

"I think that's exactly it," Jana said, "but you'll see. I'll get signed anyway. And I already have a head start since I know what a card is," she finished, hurling that final stinging comment at Cooper like a poisoned dart.

"Look, this is stupid," Cooper said, trying simultaneously to calm Jana down and figure out how everything had gone so wrong so quickly.

"It's not stupid to me," Jana told her, jumping off the bed and gathering up her books.

"That's not what I meant."

"I think it is," Jana replied venomously.

Realizing that maybe it would be best to let Jana cool down before talking about this, Cooper reached across the bed to help her with her stuff. Jana obviously didn't want Cooper's help, though, because she quickly moved to snatch the heavy book away. But it was too late. In the midst of the commotion Cooper somehow managed to hit herself painfully hard in the nose with the book as she was trying to pass it to Jana. In a matter of seconds the blood began to flow.

"Don't leave, I'll be right back," Cooper instructed, rushing from the room. She quickly grabbed a towel from the linen closet and held it to her nose, then returned to the spot where she had left Jana.

"I really don't want you to leave like this," Cooper said as the towel turned bright crimson. Her head was beginning to pound, too.

"I really don't think there's anything else to say," Jana sniffed before heading for the door. "Oh, and you might want to call Claire and tell her we won't be going to The Cupping Room after all."

After Jana flounced out the door in a huff, Cooper went back to her room to lie down, still shaken by the morning's events. She wasn't feeling very well, and she didn't know if it was from the ugly confrontation or the bump on the nose. She knew she needed to sit down. Perched precariously on the edge of her bed, she noticed that Jana had left the Josh McDowell book behind. Once she was feeling a little less lightheaded, Cooper went to check out the damage in the little silver mirror on her desk.

She was amazed to find that although the bleeding seemed to have stopped, her nose was swollen and even starting to bruise a little. *This is like a bad episode of* The

Brady Bunch! she thought miserably. Then just when she didn't think things could get any worse, she realized she had carelessly set her bloody towel on her portfolio.

Forgetting the pounding in her head, Cooper ran to the kitchen to retrieve some paper towels that she then wet under the sink. Several frantic minutes later she decided that the damage was minimal. Since the cover was black it was hard to make out the few smudges, and she was sure when it dried it would be fine. Suddenly, Cooper noticed something else—Tara's card was nowhere to be found.

"COOPER ELLIS! WHAT on earth happened to you?" her mother shrieked, waking her from a deep sleep.

"What?" Cooper groggily asked.

"You look like you ran face-first into a truck!" Mrs. Ellis replied with a note of panic still clinging to her words.

"Oh, my nose," Cooper said absently.

"Yes, your nose is right. What did you do to it?"

"I hit it with a book," Cooper explained, knowing it sounded implausible.

"It must have been some book. What did you use? The *New York Public Library Desk Reference*?"

"It was an accident," she added unnecessarily.

"Well, I would hope you weren't just sitting here beating yourself on your face on purpose!" her mother answered. "Still, however you did it, you need to go have it looked at. You might have done some permanent damage . . . and just when your modeling career was getting underway," she added fretfully.

"Thanks for your concern for my well-being," Cooper replied a little sarcastically, "but I'm not going to the doctor for a bump on the nose. I put ice on it and now I just want to rest. I feel really tired."

"That's because you probably have a concussion! You shouldn't sleep if that's the case. Now we'll have to go to the emergency room and then to a plastic surgeon! Oh, what a day," her mother lamented.

"Mom, really, I'm fine. The bump gave me a headache, that's all. I don't have a concussion and I refuse to go see a plastic surgeon. Besides, who's going to see me on a Saturday?"

"You've got a point there. Doctors keep worse hours than bankers these days, but you're not off the hook, young lady," she warned. "I plan to make some calls on Monday. If you've done some serious damage to your nose, we'll want to have it fixed as soon as possible."

"A nose job?" a disbelieving Cooper asked. "Are you talking about a nose job?" The words were barely out when she erupted into giggles, but the laughing made her nose hurt all over again, and tiny jolts of pain seemed to shoot out in a million directions from her injured facial feature.

"Ouch!" Cooper cried as she tried to stop laughing.

"You see? You're seriously hurt," her mother insisted.

"I don't agree that it's serious, but we have until Monday to keep arguing about it, so let's call a truce for right now so I can go back to sleep."

"Only if you agree to seriously consider going to see a plastic surgeon—don't forget you have a career to consider now—and you put another ice pack on your nose before taking a nap," her mother bargained.

"Fine, fine, fine," Cooper agreed, willing to say just about anything at that point. She was feeling very fuzzy suddenly. Like nothing would come into focus—neither her thoughts, nor her words, nor her mother standing over her with worry clouding her features.

"I'll get the ice," Mrs. Ellis volunteered, rushing from the room as if she were afraid her daughter would change her mind if she were given time to think about it.

"Mmm'kay," Cooper mumbled in response. She was already drifting off.

"Now, doesn't that feel better?" her mother asked after returning to Cooper's bedroom and depositing the refilled ice bag right between her eyes.

"It feels colder, that's for sure."

"Leave it on there. It will help the swelling," Mrs. Ellis instructed. Cooper knew by her tone it was no use arguing, so she curled up under her covers with the bag pressed firmly against her face.

"Now, get some rest, sweetheart, and I'll wake you in a few hours for dinner."

❄   ❄   ❄

It was dark when Cooper woke, but despite getting some rest she felt worse than when she went to sleep, as if now she needed an ice pack for her entire body. She was hot and achy, and her mouth felt like it was filled with cotton or Kleenex or something equally absorbent. In fact, her horrible thirst was the only thing that got her out of bed.

"Your nose looks a bit better," Mrs. Ellis said after Cooper managed to wobble to the kitchen. "Are you up for a little vegetarian chili?"

Cooper's stomach churned at the mere mention of it, and she shook her head emphatically from side to side.

"I can't eat anything," she insisted. "I just want something to drink."

"But you haven't eaten since breakfast! I know you—

135

you'll be in here eating ice cream or chips in an hour," her mother predicted, disapproval in her voice.

"Not this time. I honestly don't feel like I could eat anything. I just need some orange juice and I'll be fine."

"Let me feel your head."

Cooper surrendered her forehead and cheeks for her mother's scrutiny.

"Why, no wonder. You're burning up! You go right back to bed," she instructed. "I'll bring you your juice and the thermometer."

"Oh great," Cooper groaned, but she was too weak to put up much of a fight. She tried to be patient while her mother hovered over her.

"It's 102," Mrs. Ellis announced triumphantly after removing the thermometer and examining it carefully. "I told you you were sick."

"I thought I was the one who figured that out," Cooper shot back before softening a little. Her mother really did seem concerned. "I'm sure it's nothing major. I must have just caught that flu that's going around. A bunch of kids were out last week with it."

"I knew you should have gone in for a flu shot last fall. You are going to need to be much more careful about these things in the future, though. What if Yakomina gets you a job and you're sick? You can't afford to catch every little illness that passes through your school."

"It's not like I got the flu on purpose," Cooper tried to explain.

"Of course you didn't. I'm just saying you're going to have to be more careful in the future. Make sure you eat right, drink lots of water, get plenty of sleep, and wash your hands often. I bet that school is just full of germs."

"I'll keep that in mind. Now, can I have my juice before I wither away?"

"Oh! I'm sorry," Mrs. Ellis said. She was so intent on making her point that she had forgotten all about the drink she was holding in her other hand.

❊   ❊   ❊

Cooper didn't feel any better on Sunday, so she stayed home from church but was finally coherent enough to take phone calls later that night.

"So what happened to you yesterday? I thought we were going to The Cupping Room with Jana?" Claire asked when she called. "Your mom said you had the flu when I saw her at church this morning."

"Yeah, I'm sorry I didn't call you yesterday. The Cupping Room would have been out, though, even if I had felt great. Jana and I got into a little fight," Cooper explained, still wincing as she remembered the ugly misunderstanding.

"What do you mean you got into a fight?"

"She came over and I was convinced that God wanted me to talk to her about Him—you know, she had so many questions the other day in the reading group—and that that was the reason He had brought us together."

"And she got upset about that?" Claire wondered.

"Not really. I never quite got to that. She got upset because she had an agenda, too. She wanted me to help her break into modeling. I told her I didn't have any clout and kindly suggested she might be a little too short, and she accused me of not wanting her as competition in the business, then she stormed out of here."

"That's bizarre."

"That's what I thought. It gets worse, though," Cooper told her.

"You mean there's more?"

"I was helping her gather up her stuff, and I hit myself in the face with this huge modeling book she had, and now my nose is about fifty different shades of blue."

"Oh, Cooper!" Claire cried, sounding as if she was trying very hard to hold back her laughter.

"I know, I know. And feel free to go ahead and laugh. It *is* funny, especially if you could see my face."

"I guess it's a good thing you still have a fever, then, or you'd have to go to school like that tomorrow," Claire pointed out helpfully.

"I hadn't even thought that far ahead."

"Well, that's what you have me for."

"Uh-oh! My mom is standing in the doorway with the thermometer. I think that's a hint to get off the phone."

"Yeah, I guess I better go, too," Claire said. "I'll call you tomorrow night to see if you're still contagious, and if not I'll stop by."

"Thanks. I'll talk to you then. Don't have too much fun at school without me," Cooper teased.

"Don't worry, I'm sure I won't."

✳   ✳   ✳

The tenacious fever was still hanging around on Monday, but Cooper was well enough to move to the living room couch, where she could watch TV. Her mother left for work still threatening to call a plastic surgeon and set up an appointment, but Cooper decided to deal with that if and when it became a reality. In the interim, she knew she'd better call

Tara and let her know that she wouldn't be going on any calls for a few days.

She had to look the number up in the phone book because she still couldn't find Tara's card, but once she dialed she was put right through by the indifferent receptionist.

"Hey, Cooper!" Tara said, coming on the line. "This is so weird. I was just going to call and leave a message on your machine. You will never guess what happened! I have great news!" she continued enthusiastically.

"I could use some," Cooper told her. "What's up?"

"You know those two calls you went on last Friday afternoon?" Tara queried.

As if she could forget them!

"Well, the first magazine you visited wants to use you! Can you believe it? Your first call and you get the job! Do you know how rare that is?"

"Uh . . . no," Cooper stammered, unsure of how to tell her agent what she knew she had to.

"You don't sound too excited."

"I'm sorry, but I have some news of my own. How rare is it for a model to show up at her first booking with the flu and a black-and-blue nose?" Cooper asked.

"You're sick? But the shoot's not until Friday. You'll be fine by then," Tara said.

"The flu will be gone, but my nose is a mess."

"Define 'a mess' for me," Tara commanded.

"I hit it with a book and it's all bruised," Cooper volunteered.

"It's not broken, is it? Tell me it's not broken," Tara frantically asked.

"No, I mean I don't think so. It seems like it's just bruised."

"Not that that diagnosis isn't very reassuring," Tara continued, "but I want a second opinion. I'll give you the name of a doctor I want you to go see as soon as possible. He's done some work for a few of our girls."

"My mom will be so glad you agree with her," Cooper unenthusiastically responded.

"You should agree with her, too," Tara warned. "You don't want to let something like this go. Now, I'll call and set up an appointment for you this afternoon—I'll call back with the exact time—and then I'll call the magazine and see if I can stall them for a few days. I doubt we can, though. You probably lost this one."

"I'm really sorry," Cooper said. She hadn't dreamed that her clumsiness would ever cause problems for anyone but her. She silently vowed to be more careful in the future.

"I know you didn't do it on purpose. And who knows, maybe it will all work out," Tara said optimistically, but she didn't sound convinced.

❉   ❉   ❉

Later that afternoon, Cooper sat in the waiting room of the plastic surgeon's office feeling completely ridiculous. It certainly wasn't uncommon in New York City and there were even girls at school who had had their noses done, but Cooper thought it was a total waste of money.

"Cooper Ellis?" the nurse called, interrupting Cooper's reading. She was engrossed in a recent issue of *New York* magazine. *At least his subscriptions are current*, Cooper thought. *That's more than you can say for my regular doctor, who stocks decades-old copies of* Highlights *and* National Geographic.

"So you're one of Tara's girls," the doctor said as he entered the room. "It looks like you took a nasty spill."

"I had a collision with a book," Cooper sheepishly explained.

"I see. Well, let's take stock of the damage, shall we?" he proposed.

After a few minutes of poking and prodding that was only mildly uncomfortable compared to other doctor visits, Cooper was excused. As she had been insisting, it was only a bump, and by the end of the week she would look almost like her old self again, the doctor predicted. Pushing open the heavy door that led to the street, Cooper took the five short steps two at a time and thought about how relieved Tara and her mother would be. She would call and give them a full report as soon as she got home.

"Cooper?" an unsure voice asked. It was Lindsay, Jana's friend, and she must have been making her way home after school.

"I didn't realize you lived in this neighborhood," Cooper told her. She was eager to get home but forced herself to stop and make polite conversation.

"Just a block down," Lindsay volunteered, pointing to a row of brownstones in the distance. "What are you doing? I didn't see you in school."

"I've got the flu," Cooper explained. "I had a doctor's appointment, though, that's why I'm out."

"Oh," Lindsay replied, sounding confused. "I guess if you're sick I should let you get home so you can go back to bed."

"Yeah, I guess I should go," Cooper agreed. There was something strange in Lindsay's voice, but Cooper was too anxious to get home to worry too much about it. "I'll see you at school later in the week," she added as she hurried off.

Shedding her many layers of warm clothing as soon as she was inside, Cooper realized that even the mild exertion of walking to her appointment had been exhausting. After calling to report in to her mom and Tara, she curled up and took yet another nap. She still had a mild fever and was anxious to get rid of it because lying around the house like a slug was getting old.

She especially wanted to get well so that she could go out on more calls and get some more modeling jobs. Cooper really felt like she had let Tara down and was anxious to make it up to her. *If anyone will ever hire me again after this,* she worried fitfully before drifting off into a fevered sleep. She hoped she hadn't blown her big chance.

EVEN WITH ALL THE EXTRA sleep, it wasn't until Wednesday that Cooper was able to return back to school. By then her nose looked considerably better and with a little more makeup than usual the bruises weren't as noticeable. Still, people seemed to be looking at her strangely all morning. She wasn't entirely sure, but she thought maybe they were whispering about her, too.

I guess my fever's not completely gone after all, Cooper said to herself. *I'm beginning to hallucinate.*

"Hey, lab partner, can I get the homework from you?" Cooper asked Josh before class started in bio. It was good to see him again, she had to admit, even if she didn't know where things stood between him and Jana.

"Sure," he told her, sounding anything but generous.

"Thanks. I was out with the flu, and now I have a ton of catching up to do," she complained.

"The flu, huh?" he asked, looking puzzled.

"Yep. I had a 102 fever on Sunday," she volunteered, not sure why she felt she needed to offer proof but doing it all the same.

"Here are the assignments," he said, passing her his notebook without meeting her eyes. "You'll have to get the work sheet from Mr. Robbins."

"Thanks," Cooper said when she passed the notebook back after copying down the pertinent information. Before, she just thought she'd been imagining things, but people were treating her very strangely, and Josh's behavior was nothing short of cold.

At lunch things were normal, though. Cooper didn't even mind waiting in the Coke machine line. Once she finally made it out to the courtyard, she and Alex and Claire spent the period doing more catching up than eating. Her friends said they didn't notice anything strange about Cooper and agreed with her earlier assessment that she must be imagining things.

"Maybe Josh was just having a bad day," Claire said.

"And you're probably feeling self-conscious about your nose, so you think anyone you see whispering must be talking about you," Alex added.

"I'm sure you guys are right," Cooper replied, feeling silly for even bringing up her paranoid theories.

Now all she needed to explain away was why Jana and company were notably absent. In light of the incident the previous Saturday, though, Cooper hadn't really expected her to join them for lunch. She was surprised to find, however, that she hadn't eaten with Claire and Alex while Cooper had been out sick, either.

"I think she just needs some time to cool down," Claire suggested. "Things will get back to normal after the reading group tomorrow, I'm sure."

"Unless they don't come to the reading group," Cooper added.

"Oh, they'll come. They've come every week," Alex reminded her, unwilling to accept any other outcome.

"I hope so," Cooper shrugged. It was funny to think how resistant she had been to Jana and her friends bursting into her quiet, orderly life. Now, only a few weeks later, she had grown so used to having them around it seemed odd not to eat with them.

"I'm sure if we just treat her normally this whole thing will blow over," Claire said confidently. "She's probably just embarrassed that she made such a big deal about the modeling thing."

"I guess," Cooper agreed. It sounded logical, anyway. It didn't do any good to worry about it now since they'd find out soon enough. Besides, Cooper was still thirsty.

"I'm going to run inside for some juice," Cooper announced. "I'm still a little dehydrated from the flu."

"Okay, but you probably won't make it back out here before the bell rings, so you'd better take your stuff," Alex pointed out.

"You're right."

After gathering up her things, Cooper said good-bye to her friends and pushed her way back through the crowds in the cafeteria. Cookies went on sale during the last fifteen minutes of lunch, and everyone was always shoving their way in to get one of the hot, chewy treats before rushing off to class. Today was no exception, and it took Cooper ten minutes to elbow her way up to the front. She had just paid for her carton of orange juice when someone on her left crashed against her, throwing her into the person on her right.

Cooper looked up to see who owned the broad chest she found herself leaning against and almost died when she realized it belonged to none other than Micah Jacobson! Her heart was pounding furiously as she struggled to right herself. She knew her face had to be the color of a pomegranate. To her great surprise, he gently put his hands on her shoulders and steadied her before flashing her one of his heart-melting smiles.

It could have turned into one of those wonderfully romantic moments like in the movies where the guy and girl accidentally touch and his hand lingers for just a few seconds longer than necessary so that even when he takes it away you know she can still feel it there. Then their eyes lock and he delivers one of those perfect lines before taking her in his arms and kissing her.

It could have happened that way—if only Cooper weren't involved. For some reason her life didn't work like that. Instead, Micah helped her get her balance, smiled, then said, "They sure made a mess of your nose! I would have left it alone if I were you." Then he turned to his friend, who laughed as they walked away.

Cooper just stood there stunned. What was he talking about? He acted like she had chosen to have her nose look like it did, but that made no sense. Confused and upset that she had blown yet another chance with Micah, she went to geometry class and forced herself to concentrate. At least geometry made sense to her.

❄   ❄   ❄

Thursday was much of the same, but Cooper was getting used to ignoring the strange looks and hushed whispers. She had never really cared too much about what people who didn't know her thought of her, but still it was bizarre.

Gathered in the student lounge that afternoon, Cooper tried to prepare Alex for the possibility that it might be just the three of them again as far as the reading group was concerned. As far as everything was concerned, actually.

"It wasn't that bad when it was just us meeting, was it?" Cooper asked, poking Alex playfully in the ribs. "I mean, Claire and I are pretty fun all on our own, you know. Most guys would be thrilled at the prospect of spending time alone with the two of us each week."

Alex just smiled weakly. Cooper knew he appreciated them, but it was important for Alex to feel like he was making a difference. Although he wouldn't admit it, she knew he had enjoyed having Josh and Blake around so he wasn't always the only guy in the bunch. Cooper was still trying to tease Alex into a good mood when, to her amazement, Jana, Lindsay, Blake, and Anne came walking in just as they had done every other Thursday for weeks. Right on their heels was Josh.

"Sorry I'm late," Josh apologized. "I left something in my locker and had to run back."

"No problem!" Alex said enthusiastically. "Let's get started."

The others didn't say anything but chose seats on the available couches. They weren't silent long, though. As soon as Alex began the discussion, Jana interrupted.

"When are we going to be choosing a new book?"

"We're not even halfway through with this one," Alex pointed out.

"But I'm tired of this one," she practically whined. "I think it's only fair that we look at other subjects, too. Maybe we can start taking turns with this book and something else that isn't so spiritual."

"The point of the group is to look at literature that deals with theological issues, but I guess we could think about it,"

Alex acquiesced, although he was obviously disappointed.

"So you're saying we can't read something else, too?"

"I think it would be confusing to switch back and forth between books, but I'm not opposed to taking a vote on what we read next when we're done with this book," he explained.

Jana wasn't placated. "I knew it! You just want to run things the way you want and to make all the decisions yourself!" she charged. "Well, you can keep your closed-minded little reading group. I'm getting tired of it."

It was almost like a replay of Saturday at Cooper's, except this time when Jana stormed out, no one was bleeding and she had her entourage trailing behind her, which added to the effect. Only Anne looked back for a second as if she was maybe a little sorry to go.

For several minutes after she left, Cooper, Claire, and Alex couldn't do anything but stare at the empty spots on the couch, dumbfounded. When Cooper finally recovered, it was only then that she noticed not every spot was empty. Josh was still there, looking as shocked by Jana's outburst as they were.

"Why didn't you leave with your friends?" Cooper asked.

"They're not my friends," Josh corrected. "They were your friends. I just met them here at the group."

"But that first day . . . you seemed so . . . friendly, and you were sitting with her," Cooper stammered, trying to piece it all together. "You sat with her at lunch."

"I sat with *you* at lunch. Jana just happened to be there," Josh said.

"You mean you were never friends with her?" Cooper asked.

At that, Josh seemed to blush, and once again Cooper

thought she understood. "So you were *more* than friends," she said for him, sorry to have figured it out.

"No! That's not it at all. Actually, I, uh, well . . ." Now it was Josh's turn to stammer.

"You what?"

"I came to the group because I knew you were in it." He said the words fast, as if that way Cooper might not catch their full meaning. "Jana was friendly so I was friendly back, but I started joining you guys at lunch to talk to *you*." At this point he met her eyes, and it was the moment she hadn't had with Micah in the cafeteria the day before. Even better because she was sitting down, so there wasn't any chance of falling or doing anything else klutzy.

"You really wanted to get to know me?" Cooper asked, still finding it hard to believe.

"I thought I did," he said, but then his tone changed. "Now I'm not so sure."

"What do you mean?" Alex asked, jumping in to defend his friend.

"Well, I admit I came to the group because I wanted to get to know Cooper better, but I was also really interested in the reading. I've been doing some searching and studying on my own, and I know that C. S. Lewis didn't always have such a strong faith. I thought this would be a good place to ask questions and try to figure out what I believe, too."

"I hope it is," Alex replied. "If that's all, then I still don't see what the problem is."

"The problem is I thought you guys were different, but Cooper lied to me."

"I what? What are you talking about?" a flabbergasted Cooper asked.

"I thought we were becoming friends," Josh explained,

"but then you go and have a nose job, which is superficial enough, but on top of that you lie about it, telling me you had the flu when I can see the bruises on your face from the surgery."

He hadn't even finished when Cooper, Claire, and Alex began laughing so hard they had tears streaming down their cheeks.

"I don't think it's very funny," Josh said. "I mean, if your goal in life is suddenly to be Cindy Crawford and you want to get your face all cut up to do it, that's your business. But I didn't think you were as superficial as that."

Finally Cooper was able to compose herself enough to speak.

"You're right. If that's what I had done it wouldn't be funny, but I didn't have a nose job. I hit myself in the face with a book. And I really did have the flu. You can call my mom and ask her," Cooper offered.

"So what were you doing going to a plastic surgeon?" Josh asked, unwilling to drop the subject so quickly.

"How do you know about that?"

"So you admit you were there?" he asked, sounding like an interrogating officer from some police show on television.

"I went in to have the doctor make sure my nose wasn't broken after my mother and my agent insisted."

"Oh," Josh replied, his position obviously shaken.

"You still haven't told me how you knew I was there," Cooper repeated.

"Lindsay told me she saw you there. She also said that you told Jana on Saturday that you were getting your nose done because you didn't think you could get any modeling work if you didn't," he explained.

"And you believed her?" Cooper asked. Now it was her turn to be upset.

"I didn't until I saw your face yesterday and you came up with that lame story about having the flu."

"It wasn't a lame story! I really did have the flu!"

"I know that now. I didn't want to believe the rumors, but . . ."

"Rumors?" Claire hesitantly asked. "What rumors?"

"Oh, now it all makes sense!" Cooper cried as she began to pace agitatedly. "All the strange looks. The whispering. Lindsay and Jana told the whole school I got a nose job! But why would everyone believe her?"

"Um, Cooper?" Claire said gently. "Have you looked in the mirror lately? That's why they would believe her. Who would think you could have possibly done that much damage to yourself?"

"I guess I should have after seeing what you did to our poor worm in biology!" Josh teased.

At that, they all began to laugh—even Josh.

16

WHEN SHE GOT HOME there was a message from Tara on the machine asking Cooper to call her as soon as she got in. Cooper couldn't help wondering if maybe Yakomina was going to drop her before she even really got started. Not that she would blame them. They couldn't make any money off of a model who couldn't work. But when she returned the call, she was pleasantly surprised to find that Tara had good news instead.

"I don't know what you did to win over that editor, but the magazine wants to use you for an even bigger job and it doesn't shoot for two weeks! Do you have any idea how lucky you are?"

"Not really, but I get the impression you're going to tell me."

"You're right about that! Most editors would forget about a newcomer like you if you weren't available the first time they asked, but they said they thought you had a 'certain naïveté' they were looking for and that they were willing to wait for you."

"Now, *that* I have no problem believing!" Cooper said before telling Tara all about the card mix-up. With being sick all weekend and her injured nose, she had forgotten to fill her in earlier. "A 'certain naïveté' is exactly what I have, although I never thought it would get me work, especially in this business."

"In that case, maybe I shouldn't bother to get cards printed up for you. You might get more work your way," Tara laughed.

"Don't you dare!" Cooper told her. "I don't need any help making a fool of myself!"

"I'm just kidding. I already had the cards done up, and you can come pick them up tomorrow if you want," Tara suggested. "That would give me a chance to get a look at that nose for myself and see how it's healing."

"Whatever you say, boss."

"Oh, and one last thing while I've got you on the line. Did you happen to give my name to any of your friends? I had someone call yesterday who was interested in modeling. She used your name to get past the receptionist."

"No, I haven't given your name to anyone," Cooper said. "Didn't she tell you who she was?"

"She wouldn't say. She wanted to come in personally and show me some pictures."

Realization suddenly dawned on Cooper. "I think I have a pretty good idea who it was now, but I didn't give her your name. I think she took your card from my room. I'm sorry if she caused any trouble," Cooper apologized.

"No big deal," Tara told her dismissively. "I've had girls go to much greater lengths than that to try to get a modeling contract. You'd be amazed."

"Well, it won't happen again," Cooper vowed.

"Fine. I'll see you and that troublesome nose of yours tomorrow," Tara finished.

"Okay, then. Bye."

❄   ❄   ❄

Friday was a strangely wonderful day—and not just be-cause it was the start of the weekend. Cooper felt a little awk-ward in biology after Josh's admission the day before, but it was a nice awkward and she smiled shyly at him as she took her seat.

"Have you talked to Alex yet today?" he asked her as soon as she sat down.

"Not really. Just 'hi' between classes," she replied.

"So he didn't tell you I went over to his house last night after the reading group?"

"No," Cooper told him, unsure of what he was getting at. It was nice that he and Alex were becoming friends, but what was the big deal?

"We talked for hours," Josh continued cryptically. "Mostly about God and our faith and stuff. He's really easy to talk to."

"*Our* faith?" Cooper asked.

"Yes," Josh smiled, his eyes shining. "It was like it all fi-nally made sense, God sending His Son to die for me. That was a huge sacrifice."

"The biggest," Cooper agreed.

"Well, if I'm that important to Him, then it follows that He should be that important to me. I mean, I don't know of any-body else who's willing to die for me, so I figured there is obviously something to this Christianity thing. God's defi-nitely different to be willing to go to such lengths to get my attention."

"I won't argue with you on that one," Cooper said.

"And you and Claire and Alex are different. You're really good friends who, you know, take care of one another instead of just looking out for yourselves like a lot of people at this school. That got my attention, too."

"I'm not always the greatest friend," Cooper corrected, wondering for the millionth time if there was something she could have done differently with Jana. If there was some way she could have maybe been a better example of God's unconditional love.

"I'm not saying you never make mistakes, but at least you try," Josh said.

"Yes, I certainly do that," she agreed with a smile. "Sometimes too hard." She knew she had pushed with Jana, trying to force something that wasn't there. She had just been so sure that she knew what God wanted. Now all of a sudden she didn't have a clue, and she hated not knowing how things were going to turn out, not knowing what to expect.

Josh walked with her down to the cafeteria after class and even waited with her in the long line at the Coke machine. As they stood there moving only millimeters at a time, she noticed Jana, Lindsay, and Blake across the cafeteria. The latter two were hanging a huge poster while Jana was standing in front supervising. The sign advertised a new film discussion group. Cooper couldn't say she was surprised, but as she saw Jana bossing her friends around, needing so much to be in control of every situation, she felt sad. Sad for Jana and sad for herself.

For so long she had tried to keep everything the same, to control her world and her friends and her life, but it didn't work. She had no idea what was going to happen with the reading group, with her modeling career, with Josh, but suddenly, for the first time in her life, it didn't seem quite so important. Someone knew what was going to happen, and He wouldn't let her down. She wondered if Jana would ever come to that same understanding. She didn't think so, but then she corrected herself. She honestly didn't know what God had planned for Jana. All she could do was pray for her, which was probably what she should have been doing more of from the beginning.

"Are you going to put some quarters in or do you usually just stare at the machine and drinks pop out?" Josh asked.

"Huh? Oh, sorry," Cooper said. She was so lost in thought, she hadn't even realized it was her turn. Josh was nice about it, though. He didn't make her feel clumsy or ab-sentminded, and she was excited about what he had shared with her in biology class. She wished she could do something to commemorate the day, and then it hit her. As soon as she bought the drinks, she sent Josh on ahead.

"I just need to get something," she told him, handing over the cans. "Why don't you take these out to Claire and Alex, and I'll be right there. I promise."

Josh made his way through the throngs of Hudson High students, and she watched until he was well into the court-yard before getting in line at the junk food window. It was almost as long as the drink line, but she didn't mind. It was a beautiful sunny day out, and as she began to let go a little, to surrender some control, she felt like the sun was begin-ning to shine inside her as well.

Carrying her purchases out to her friends, she joined them at their table. Before pulling out her lunch, she opened the twin packages of chocolate cupcakes she'd bought and gave one each to Claire, Alex, and Josh.

When they gave her puzzled looks in return, she simply said, "Happy spiritual birthday!" and lifted her cupcake up toward Josh in a toast. Only then did understanding begin to dawn on the group.

"Happy spiritual birthday," Claire and Alex added, smiling warmly.

"Sorry, I didn't have any birthday candles stashed in my locker," Cooper explained to Josh when it was quiet again.

"No problem," he told her, flashing her a smile that she felt all the way to her insides. Then just when she didn't think things could get any better, Josh leaned in close and whispered a throaty "thanks" into her ear before giving her arm an affectionate squeeze. He seemed genuinely touched by her small gesture.

So she didn't know what lay ahead. *For once in my life that doesn't matter*, Cooper thought, popping the last of the celebratory cupcake in her mouth. Surrounded by friends and with so many exciting possibilities facing her, she felt sure that she—and God—were ready for whatever might come next.

THANKS TO MY FAMILY and friends for putting up with all my endless conversations about Cooper's imaginary world. Also to my D-group (sophomores already?!?), the OH! gang, and my CCM friends. I have a hard time remembering what my life was like before you. Finally to Janet Kobobel Grant, agent extraordinaire.

Young Adult Fiction Series From
Bethany House Publishers
(Ages 12 and up)

———⊶⊷———

CEDAR RIVER DAYDREAMS • by Judy Baer
Experience the challenges and excitement of high
school life with Lexi Leighton and her friends.

GOLDEN FILLY SERIES • by Lauraine Snelling
Tricia Evanston races to become the first female jockey
to win the sought-after Triple Crown.

JENNIE MCGRADY MYSTERIES • by Patricia Rushford
A contemporary Nancy Drew, Jennie McGrady's
sleuthing talents bring back readers again and again.

LIVE! FROM BRENTWOOD HIGH • by Judy Baer
The staff of an action-packed teen-run news show ex-
plores the love, laughter, and tears of high school life.

THE SPECTRUM CHRONICLES • by Thomas Locke
Adventure awaits readers in this fantasy series set in
another place and time.

SPRINGSONG BOOKS • by various authors
Compelling love stories and contemporary themes
promise to capture the hearts of readers.

UNMISTAKABLY COOPER ELLIS • by Wendy Lee Nentwig
Laugh and cry with Cooper as she strives to balance
modeling, faith, and life at her Manhattan high school.

WHITE DOVE ROMANCES • by Yvonne Lehman
Romance, suspense, and fast-paced action for teens
committed to finding pure love.